ANGELS MARK

Natalie Buske Thomas

Disclaimer: This book is a work of fiction. All events and dialog are for entertainment purposes only and do not necessarily represent the author's views.

ISBN: 0966691962
ISBN-13: 978-0966691962

DEDICATION

To my family, who believes in me

AUTHOR'S WORK

The Serena Wilcox Mysteries

Angels Mark 2011
Covert Coffee 2012
Bluebird Flown 2013
Project Scarecrow 2013
Ruby Red 2014
Future Beyond 2014
Project Willow 2014
Downward Spiral 2015

And prequel novellas: *Gene Play* 1998, *Virtual Memories* 1999, *Camp Conviction* 2000

Other Books:

Fender (The 10 Chapters Series), Thriving in a Hateful World, Ramen Noodles and Hot Dogs, Nice Authors Finish Last, Faith According to You, We are the Angels that He Sends", The Miracle Dulcimer, The Magic Camera, Grandpa Smiles, Nana Plays

For a complete list of Natalie Buske Thomas' works, including her oil paintings, please visit her website.

NatalieBuskeThomas.com

SERENA WILCOX MYSTERIES

BOOK ONE

ANGELS MARK

By Natalie Buske Thomas

CHAPTER 1

She made X's in her mashed potatoes with her fork, staring at her plate without really seeing the food. All around her was the clatter and the chatter of people dining in groups large and small, huddled under the stained glass domed lights that adorned the ceiling above each cozy table. She was conspicuously alone in a large mid-priced chain restaurant in a suburb just outside of Minneapolis.

Parents donned bibs on hungry toddlers. Some fawned all over Baby, some were embarrassed by Baby's noisy demands, and the rest ignored Baby, despite glaring looks from nearby tables. Friends shared deep-fried appetizer platters, each group with an obvious identity: co-workers blowing off steam, girls' night out, birthday party.

Couples clicked sparkling wine glasses; most pretended to share intimacy while distracted by other things. A few couples shared a real moment, with some moments more fleeting than others. Children bounced through the aisles on their way to and from the restrooms, occasionally led by a parent.

Tables with booth seating, running along every wall and tucked into every corner, were fully occupied by smiling people. The remaining tables, with traditional seating, were scattered throughout the middle of the restaurant and wedged in wall spaces too small for the booths. That was where she was sitting, the third table from the kitchen doors, hugging the wall.

"May I get you something?" said Bryce, a local college student who had recently taken this job waiting tables three nights a week. His tuition was paid for by his parents, books were covered by paternal grandparents, and clothes were gifted by his maternal grandparents. Aunts and uncles pitched in dorm and food costs. He worked solely to sustain his partying habits, which were substantial.

Seemingly never hung-over, over-stressed, or fatigued, his ever-present smile showed a history of good orthodontics and tooth whitening. Bryce's fresh good looks, topped with thick sandy locks, often netted him big tips from female diners -- but not from this one. This one didn't even look at him.

"Oh, no thanks," she said. "Wait, actually, yes. I'd like the hot fudge sundae cake. With whipped cream, but no nuts, please." She raised the glossy dessert menu and tapped her finger on the picture of the "Chocolate Lover's Deluxe Fudge Sundae Cake" special, complete with red cherry on top. The price was not special, but she wasn't thinking about cost.

"Sure," he said, his smile cranked up to full wattage. He turned away from her table quickly and merged into the swarm of patrons coming down the long carpeted aisle, his checkerboard-patterned shirt still visible until he reached the swinging kitchen doors. He should have collided with a female server, but somehow gracefully skated around her at the last possible second. The trays full of Buffalo wings she was balancing survived in defiance of all the laws of physics.

I probably made him feel uncomfortable, a woman sitting alone at a table large enough for six people. What on earth am I doing here? She sipped her soft drink slowly. How long could she make this evening stretch out? Eventually she would run out of room in her stomach. Then she would have to leave the warm restaurant with its pizzeria-like scent of garlic, and its competing craving-inducing smell of frying oil, its too-early Christmas music soundtrack competing cheerfully with the din, and its staff of people paid to be friendly. She would have to go home, except there wasn't a home to go to.

She had taken care of that late last night when she lit a red glitter taper candle and then deliberately tipped it onto a stack of piano sheet music – a gentle tap of the candlestick holder and down it went, candle and all. The paper caught fire within seconds and she watched the edges of each page from the recital version of "Let it Be" curl, blacken, and smolder before crumpling and disappearing into the fire. Soon everything else on the coffee table was ablaze.

She stood there watching the flames for what felt like hours. After the fire consumed the sheet music, an L.L.Bean catalog, an old electric bill and most of a Grisham novel, it licked at the wood of the coffee table. She worried that the fire would exhaust itself before catching on to the table, but the flames eventually took root in its mahogany frame. From then on, the fire progressed slowly.

As hard as it was to be patient, she couldn't hurry it along. She could only stand by helplessly, hoping that it would pick up power and speed, spreading itself until the whole room was engulfed. She waited; her feet hurting from standing so long, her bladder full, and her throat dry.

When the room finally began to fill with smoke, she went downstairs where her bags were packed and ready for her on her favorite chair. She slung the oversized backpack over her right shoulder, grabbed one bag with her left hand, and wheeled the third bag with her right hand. She waited a few more minutes, making sure the fire was spreading throughout the house.

She heard the thud of something falling in the kitchen and felt certain that the rest of the house would be gone within the next hour or so. She took one last look around, at the picture frames on the mantel: her daughters, her son, her husband. She set her bags down and opened one of the glass walk-out patio doors. She put a coat on, but didn't take the time to zip the front. Then she grabbed her bags and left the house for the last time.

~~ ~~

"Would you like a refill?" Bryce set the dessert in front of her and reached for her glass. The trapped body heat in the restaurant had already melted the leftover ice cubes in her nearly empty beverage.

"Yes, please," she said. Why not? She had nowhere to go. She was amazed that she could have any appetite at all, but she *had* gone for almost 48 hours without much to eat or drink. She craved comfort foods and sugar.

"I'll be right back," he said, disappearing again into the steady stream of Friday night diners, many of whom were now waiting in line to be seated. Dirty slush had been tracked in from their feet, puddling into a gray sludge on the carpet. The crowd was thickening now, and the empty chairs around her table had been added to adjoining tables after the perfunctory polite inquiry, "Is this seat taken?" She shook her head no after each request. Five requests later, she was sitting in the only chair left at the table.

She ate her dessert methodically. She removed the cherry and ate that first, returning the stem to her plate. Then she moved on to the sides and bottom. When the cake was nearly gone, she saved the biggest dollop of whipped cream to go down with the last bite of chocolate. She spent the next two minutes people-watching while draining the rest of her second soda.

When Bryce returned, she asked for coffee. He didn't express any surprise, but surely by now he was starting to wonder when she would ever leave the restaurant, especially with tables in high demand. His restraint was motivated by pity, great customer service, or apathy – she didn't know, but she felt blessed that he didn't try to hurry her along on this starry Minnesota night.

She altered her coffee with two creams and five sugar packets, stirring the sweet slurry until it became the caramel color she was looking for. She held the orange cup with both of her cool hands wrapped around it and lifted the coffee to her face, letting the aromatic steam warm her. Nursing the coffee confection for ten minutes, she breathed in the comforting smell and allowed herself to remember a cup of coffee she had five years ago.

~~ ~~

Tom had been grinding coffee beans. The shrill whine from the high-decibel grinder masked all other sounds. After he shut the grinder off both of them were startled by the new sound breaking the silence: the phone was ringing, and was probably on its third or fourth ring. He glanced at the caller-ID screen and said, "Ball State."

"Again?" she shrugged. Every weekend Ball State had been calling their alumni, presumably to raise funds for the university. She was relieved that the call was not one they needed to answer. She considered turning the phone's ringer off, but focused her sleepy mind back on to coffee. Normally she didn't have a cup of coffee so late in the day, but life was changing fast and a lot of things were going to be different.

Tom pushed the powdered creamer in her direction. She reached beyond him to open the silverware drawer and pulled out a spoon. She scooped sugar out of the counter canister, spilling some granules on the counter, adding more sugar to the crystallized ring around the canister. A few seconds later, she was sipping coffee that was brewed too strong for her. She added a spray of canned whipped cream. Tom took the whipped cream and added some to his coffee too.

Both stood in the kitchen, leaning into the cluttered and crumb-littered island counter, silently sipping coffee. The quiet was unnerving. Each of them expected the silence to be shattered at any moment, but the phone did not ring again.

The frigid air outside froze sound itself. Nothing was stirring. They looked at each other at the same time, and laughed softly, a laugh devoid of mirth. Laughter was nothing more to them at that moment than a nervous tic.

Tom drained the rest of his coffee and added his "Real Men Do Diapers" mug, a leftover from when they'd had babies in the house, to the dirty dishes in the dishwasher. He walked behind her and put his arms around her. She rested the back of her head on his shoulder. Her dark hair, naturally a "nutmeg" shade according to color charts, looked even darker next to Tom's short blonde locks.

They were physical opposites in other ways too. He was long in the torso, short on legs. Serena was short in the torso, long on legs. Both were on the short end of the height scale though, and fit together as a cute couple, friendly and wholesome. Nice. Sexy and powerful were not adjectives assigned to the pair of them, but they felt that way when they were alone together, especially when life had them feeling on edge, either because little things were not going their way, or, like now, because things were completely unsettled.

Serena drank in Tom's cologne and tried to quiet her energy, but she quickly grew restless with the embrace. Her back hurt from the slight pressure of Tom leaning on her. The feeling was mutual: Tom was antsy to pull away so that he could pace the kitchen. Each waited a polite moment before pulling away from each other simultaneously. This was how they were; married long enough to finish each other's thoughts and move in synchronized steps without any words at all.

"They're saying something," said Tom. He ran into the living room, grabbed the remote and turned up the volume. They planted their stance a few feet away from the large TV. They were too keyed up to sit or move, their bodies trembling and their stomachs in knots. Blinking their eyes felt foreign, swallowing saliva was difficult over their thick dry throats, and their every breath felt labored.

They felt united with all of America, and with people from all over the world, as they all watched the events unfold on live television together – the shared passive observance of tragedy that would bind them all together forever, and would alter future generations with every passing second. This was that moment in time that they had all dreaded, that time in history that populations had feared for decades. It had arrived, and it was every bit as monumental as every clichéd movie Serena had ever seen, and it was punctuated by live reporting on television.

The news anchors' faces would be etched in their collective brains as the faces everyone turned to for reassurance and information. New stars were born, as lesser-known reporters stepped up in stations outside of New York. The current face on the screen belonged to Brandon Swenson of Minneapolis.

We are hearing reports of a single blast from what we now know is a nuclear bomb that was a direct hit to New York City and we are just now, we are just now hearing, we are hearing that Washington D.C. has also been hit. The President is in an undisclosed location. The President has been confirmed to be safe. I repeat that, at this time, there has been no threat to the President.

We are now learning of another blast. There is another blast on Philadelphia. Yes, we are just now learning of another hit. The affected cities are now L.A., New York, Washington, D.C., and this just in, Philadelphia. We have yet to learn who is taking responsibility for these attacks. Where will it all end, America?

We are reporting live from our sister stations in Minneapolis and Chicago. I regret that many of our colleagues were in the affected cities at the time of the blast. This is a dark day for America, a very dark day.

Tom turned the closed captioning on and muted the sound. The reporters, and guest experts, were saying the same information in a desperate loop of nothing-new-to-report during the climax of the world's worst crisis.

He turned the sound back on when the footage cut back to Brandon Swenson. Brandon looked way too young and inexperienced to handle this moment in history. The baby-faced reporter read frantically from the teleprompter, not bothering to conceal the emotion from his voice.

We are now expecting to hear from the President. He will be speaking from the James R. Thompson center in Chicago within the hour, where people are already gathering in the streets in unprecedented numbers. A strong police presence and secret service detail is already in place, and the Army National Guard has also been called in.

The President is requesting that Americans not panic. He is asking that people stay by their televisions and radios and wait for information. He is expected to announce a national registry to locate missing persons, and to reassure the American people that the United States of America is containing this crisis and will make our country safe again.

The President is likely to address the United States' response to the attacks. It is unclear if the President will be taking questions at this time.

The two of them sat there, sunk into their respective lounge chairs, saying nothing for several long minutes. Tom muted the TV, but they continued to read the closed-captioning as it parroted the same information.

When Serena finally broke the silence, she and Tom entered a calm discussion as if nothing unusual was happening. They began rambling and musing, spinning conspiracy theories, as if retelling the plot of a favorite suspense movie. There was nothing about their conversation or demeanor to suggest that the nation was on the brink of World War III, Armageddon, or the end of the world as they knew it.

Each of them had an awareness of their behavior being completely off rhythm with the shocking events devastating the planet with each passing second, but neither could shake off their state of denial. So there they sat; the two of them as placid as if they were talking about the weather.

~~ ~~

A sudden shriek from a toddler at a neighboring table snapped Serena back to the present moment. She realized that she could not linger at the restaurant table a minute more. She couldn't eat another bite, couldn't drink another beverage. Besides, if she stayed any longer, her stalling would turn into loitering, drawing attention to her. It was time to leave this warm safe haven, with its comforting babble of people noise, and her personal server whose job it was to make small talk with her, and hit the road again.

She left a generous tip on the table- in cash, of course- donned her winter coat, and made her way toward the lobby, which was empty. Everyone was snuggled inside while she was headed outside.

Cheery pine swags and artificial holly bade her farewell, a basket of candy canes invited her to take a parting gift, and in the relative quiet of the lobby, Christmas music filled her ears. *The thrill of hope, the weary world rejoices, from yonder breaks a new and glorious morn…*

CHAPTER 2

Near the exit door she stepped around the puddles of slush the best she could, but the cold and slippery tile had few clean patches left to step on. Opening the heavy door, the outside chill did not hit her right away. The time spent in the cozy restaurant had heated her body like a charcoal brick – each human body connecting and keeping each other warm. Her body retained this heat as she walked down the cleared sidewalk, admiring the twinkling lights of the holiday decorations.

When she reached the end of the walk and stepped into the shadows of the parking lot, she felt no comfort from the street lights. The charcoal glow that kept her warm as she walked down the sidewalk was already gone. She felt the frigid air settle deep into her winter coat, covering her with a blanket of cold. She regretted wearing the pants she had on, some type of nylon blend. The cold was easily passing through the fabric, chilling her legs to the point of numbness.

After unlocking the minivan's doors with her electronic key, she paused to look up. Glorious stars sparkled brightly in the cold, cold, blue-black night sky. The moon shimmered. This, the way the sky looked, was the beauty that she associated with the frightening sensation of deep dense air in her lungs, making her every breath a struggle against the heavy cold air. *Beauty and fear; hope and despair.*

The van started up on the second attempt. She was lucky the thing still ran at all. It wasn't much to look at: a 1997 white-with-rust Plymouth minivan with both rear hubcaps missing. There was a deepening crack in the windshield from when a rock had hit the glass.

Inside the minivan was not any better. The van had a malfunctioning electrical panel and every warning light on the dash blinked incessantly until after the engine had been running for about two minutes. After that, the dash lights magically went out. Tom had a mechanic look at it, but he couldn't find anything wrong, so they learned to ignore the problem with the lights, forgetting all about it.

In addition to the panel malfunction, the passenger's side window no longer went up or down. If Tom or Serena forgot to warn friends and family not to use the window, they would be forced to drive with the window open until they could safely stop. One person would then hold the close button while another person stood on the other side of the door, pressing firmly down on the window until the window started moving upward. This procedure often took several minutes.

These quirks she had learned to deal with, as long as the van still ran. But now she was worried. Why hadn't they kept up with the maintenance issues, or pressed harder to get the electrical panel fixed? She would have a hard time buying another vehicle if this one failed, and she couldn't risk interacting with a mechanic to fix the minivan if it failed, *if* it was even possible to resurrect it. All she could do was hope that the minivan would hold up for as long as she needed to use it.

Serena adjusted her seat as far forward as she could. She had forgotten to adjust the seat after Tom had driven the van, which made the twenty mile trip to the restaurant like driving a go-cart, her leg extended its full length to reach the gas pedal. Long gone was the little red car she had when she and Tom were first married. Now she shared the mini-van, or at least she did when life was normal.

She sat for a second or two and noticed that her breath formed a perfect cloud in the ice-box interior of the van. The heater was chugging away but she didn't feel any comfort from it yet. She continued to obsess about the mini-van, and how the crack on the windshield looked slightly longer than it was the last time she studied it; scarcely feeling the cold steering wheel with her bare hands, until she remembered the fleece-lined driving gloves she had in her coat pocket.

She put her gloves on, slowly, concentrating on each finger as it went inside the gloves. *Enough already! Pull yourself together and get out of here!* She gripped the wheel with determination, put her foot on the pedal, now within a comfortable leg-reach from her body, and drove the van out of the restaurant parking lot.

There was no turning back. Farther and farther she drove, past suburban housing developments with their hundreds of tasteful white Christmas lights lining identical roofs on identical houses, past vacant department stores bearing illuminated icy parking lots, past gas stations with a surplus of frozen cut pine trees leaning against quick-stop stores, and past banks displaying the current outside temperature of -17, not including "wind chill factor".

After a long stretch on the freeway the steady blur of traffic lights, holiday lights, street lights, and headlights tapered off. Serena slowed to the 30mph speed limit to meet up with the wreath-lined streets of the small town of Cannon Falls, Minnesota, which was a frequent pit-stop for truckers driving between the Twin Cities and Rochester. The town, with a population of around 4,000, had benefited from media attention after former United States President Obama selected Cannon Falls for a town hall meeting stop on his tour of the Midwest states. The presidential stop helped The Old Market Deli become a tourist attraction, due to its framed photographs of the former president ordering a "Tom Turkey" sandwich. To this day, the chair he sat in was marked with duct tape.

As she reached the only traffic light in the town, she stopped in front of a multicolored canopy of Christmas lights draped across the intersection. She studied the lights as she waited for the light to change. She could almost hear the crackling of ice crystals as the lights swayed. She tracked the rocking motion of the lights with her eyes, eyes dry and bloodshot from fatigue and the hot air from the minivan's heater. She willed her eyes to stay open. She looked in the rearview mirror. Her green eyes had so much red around them that Serena thought, *I have Christmas eyes. Oh no, I'm getting slap-happy. I need to snap out of it. I still have twenty miles left to go.*

One second, two seconds, three seconds. There were no other vehicles around. It was tempting to ignore the red light, but she couldn't risk a traffic violation, or the unlikely event that a car would come out of nowhere and zip through the intersection, colliding with her, so she waited for what felt like a long time but probably wasn't. She surveyed the downtown area, noticing lights on behind one of the storefront windows: chiropractor Fletcher was tending to an emergency after-care patient who had been rear-ended in an auto accident an hour earlier. All other buildings were dark. Finally the light changed and she was on her way.

She drove past Cannon Falls' post office and grocery store, which shared a common parking lot, and past its only public school complex; all grades K-12 were taught among the two brick buildings located at the edge of town, just inside city limits.

Earlier in the day the area was a hub of activity with teen drivers leaving school, parents picking up students, and orange-yellow buses lined up along the full length of the sidewalk. Now the area was deserted, lit only by security lights.

As the school faded away from view, she passed St. Ansgar's Lutheran Church, a church that held both traditional and contemporary worship services, and served as an emergency shelter for the neighboring school district for emergencies that, post 9/11, included terrorist attacks and bomb threats. Serena idly wondered if the church had been full of school children on that horrible day that was the catalyst for everything else that happened.

St. Ansgar's was the last sight of Cannon Falls -- and the last sign of civilization. After she drove by the outlying residential areas, and a few rural properties, nothing greeted her as she maneuvered the windy roads and icy bridges between Cannon Falls and Red Wing.

Tangled leaf-less trees, *Halloween trees*, filled the bluffs on both sides of the desolate road, not a home in sight -- nothing but the moonlight that bounced off the snow and provided an eerie violet-white glow that illuminated the darkness. Other than the moonlight, which was partially obscured by cloud cover coming in, it was pitch black, the kind of blackness that only the most rural areas are steeped in.

There were no other vehicles, except for one abandoned car in a ditch. The minivan's headlights were the only artificial light source. Serena struggled to keep her eyelids from closing.

Exhaustion washed over her in waves of dizziness and her vision took on an altered-state quality. With no visible traffic lines on the road, she wasn't sure if she was weaving all over the center line or if she was precariously hugging the edge. In some places, if she ran off the road, it would be a sharp dive off an elevated area and into a ravine. It was hard to tell what type of landscape lurked around each bend, over each hill, in the low-lying valleys in between.

She had been driving about ten miles and she was now way outside any easily known physical address. Some of the farm residents in this area had a Minneapolis area code, a Goodhue zip code, and belonged to the Cannon Falls school district. In other words, it was fairly easy for them to fall off the grid -- even the GPS found their existence difficult to locate—which was why Serena was almost home.

A few more rotations of the minivan's tires over the snow and ice covered gravel road, and she would be there. The driveway was long, and uphill, so she fretted that she would never get the van up the hill. She applied pressure to the accelerator pedal and heard nothing but the tell-tale squeal of tires that were spinning without traction. She blinked instant tears away. She was home now. No reason to break down.

A light went on in the house on top of the hill. She saw silhouettes moving in the windows: one, two, three, and a small fourth. Then a switch was turned on and dozens of evergreens, tall and short, lit up in red, green, gold, and white. The wintery hill was a Christmas wonderland welcoming her home.

That was when she lost it. Tears, nearly freezing upon impact, streamed down her cheeks. She sat there in the minivan at the bottom of the driveway, sobbing, her driving gloves still clutching the steering wheel, for what felt like ages. She'd lost all sense of the passage of time; she didn't know if she sat there for two minutes, five, or ten.

After her meltdown subsided, she pulled herself together and backed into the road to give the minivan a running start to make it up the hill. Gravity got her past the slick spots – fast. Going down was easy.

It took her three attempts, but she finally made it up the driveway, and into the garage, where the door had already been opened for her. After she parked the minivan and switched off the engine, Serena dug for a tissue in her purse and hurriedly blew her nose while looking at herself in the pull-down visor mirror. She wasn't going to win any pageants tonight, but it was hard to tell that she had been crying. Her face was already red from the cold, and her eyes were bloodshot from fatigue. Her meltdown was hardly noticeable – she was ready to reunite herself with her family.

~~ ~~

After Tom and the kids tackled her in a group hug, Tom said, "I was about to go look for you. Why didn't you call? It's a disposable phone, and no one is looking for us anyway."

"I misplaced the phone."

Tom laughed. He knew how often she misplaced things. "I'm glad you're home." He gave her a kiss on the forehead and pried Rebecca from her death grip around Serena's waist. "Let Mommy take her coat off."

Serena draped her slightly damp coat over a kitchen chair and all of them sat around the table. Carrie had made sugar cookies earlier that afternoon and Rebecca had decorated one especially for her, a heart shaped cookie with French vanilla frosting and red candy sprinkles. Tom had both wine and coffee on hand, not knowing which one she would want. Samuel had learned a new song on his guitar to play for her homecoming. Cookies, beverages and music were offered to her all at once. After the flurry of excitement died down, the kids went to bed while the adults lingered in the kitchen for a few minutes longer.

There they sat, knowing their actions were irreversible. Two days ago Tom had finished up his last day of work – not that his boss, or any of his co-workers, *knew* it was his last day. He made sure that he worked a regular full day, with nothing in his attitude showing what he was up to. Meanwhile, he had been making preparations for weeks. He sold personal items using anonymous online auctions, stockpiling all the cash he could. He thought it was very unlikely that anyone would look for them, or that anyone would look into their "deaths" very deeply. Still, he was careful.

He was fairly confident that the house fire would be ruled an accident without a second thought. He had made sure that the gasoline container was staged to look as if he had been working on repairing a broken snow blower and made the tragic mistake of using the mud room as a workshop. The mud room was attached to the living space of the house. If the fire spread as they imagined it would, it was only a matter of time before the house fire created by the fallen candle in the living room would spread to the mud room, igniting the open drum of gasoline. Their only concern was that the fire needed to reach the gas before someone noticed the fire and called 911. Some of their plans were entirely out of their control, but they had a good feeling it would all work out.

From the beginning of their adventure, when Serena had been up all night looking things up on the Internet, things had fallen neatly into place. It only took a single phrase typed into a search engine ("Help me disappear") for Serena to find an underground society, known as the off-the-grid network. Next, she looked up the term "off-the-grid", and found a reference for people who wanted to live independently of public utilities, go green, and have less dependency on government. But extremists going off-the-grid, or just "off-grid", wanted to hide from the government; most likely for paranoid reasons, or to breed a militia clan. While the latter sounded scary, off-grid groups helped their members fall off the radar.

Serena posted a message to the off-grid forum, and within ten minutes heard back from a spokesperson from Off-grid-ghost, a grassroots organization which sounded like a human smuggling ring. Tom joined the group too, and by the end of the week, they'd both told their story. Off-grid-ghost immediately offered them a house where they could hide, an old farm house on a leftover slice of Minnesota farm land, completely obscured from the road. All they wanted in return was $10,000 cash and an agreement to keep their organization secret. Rent was to be paid through Off-grid-ghost: landlord and tenant were forbidden to know each other, although both were required to be members of the network.

The house was selected because records of the dwelling and property were from so long ago that no one would find them without knowing exactly what to look for, and maybe not even then. Archived paper records were often lost or destroyed from the perils of long term storage, and no one had bothered to go back far enough to digitize the records. Chances were good that there was no trace of this house existing, which qualified the location for endorsement by Off-grid-ghost, said their spokesman.

So far, everything was going according to plan, but Tom and Serena were both nervous about falling in with a radical organization like Off-grid-ghost. Yet what choice did they have if they didn't know how to disappear on their own?

It was only because they were computer savvy that they were able to learn about the underground off-the-grid network; and that was where their escape-plotting skills ended. They had no current passports and there wasn't enough time to obtain them. They didn't know what else to do, so they turned to what was, in their minds, a whack-job fringe group to help them hide. Tom and Serena considered themselves to be normal people, who just happened to find themselves in extraordinary circumstances. How could they explain their actions in a way that would not make them look crazy?

The off-grid plan was the only plan they had, so they had to trust that it would work. They weren't even sure what to wish for: was it better if nothing bad happened, and they messed up their lives for no reason? Or was it better to be "right", and not crazy? How could it be that two college educated people from suburbia would be so paranoid as to stage their deaths so that they could hide from their own government, dragging their three children with them?

They could analyze this over and over, but in the end they had only two choices: ignore the warning they believed to be true, or comply with what the government wanted. Always people of action when they believed in something, they felt they had no other option. So even though they knew very little about Minnesota, they committed to the plan right away. It was a place to hide. Hide and wait to see what would happen.

CHAPTER 3

Paul greeted General Gustavo Marino with a hearty handshake. Gustavo accepted the gesture, but kept his eyes focused on the back of President John William's gray head, which was fast slipping away to the end of Gustavo's imaginary leash. Gustavo ended the handshake quickly, and then moved forward in the procession, without ever really looking at Paul. Paul mentally shrugged his shoulders – it wasn't important to his plan to be seen.

As Paul fell back from the entourage and let the media pass him by, he watched the President's well-tailored pin-stripe suit disappear into the crowd on the tarmac. He kept up as best he could from a distance, but he hoped he could close the gap before the President got on the plane. He wanted a closer look at the man who was the President of the Liberty Union, which was comprised of the East Coast states (the ones still inhabitable anyway), the Southern states, and much of the eastern Midwest, a union otherwise known as "The Free States".

Paul caught a break when President John Williams agreed to answer questions from a handful of reporters. Everyone knew that what this really meant was that Williams had a speech prepared, probably a long-winded one. Paul settled into a comfortable standing posture. While his view was mostly obstructed by the crowd and the mob of security detail around Williams, Paul would have plenty of time to study the man, while he himself went completely unnoticed. He turned on his cell phone to start recording. He planned to show the footage to Clyde later that night.

A surfer-boy aide with a perfect smile set up a portable podium right there on the tarmac and donned it with a fabric covering depicting the Liberty Union seal. Before the aide had given the final straightening tug on the fabric, President Williams placed himself in a rehearsed photogenic position behind the podium. He catered to the crowd for a few minutes before rattling off a speech that would make the speech writer, unknown to anyone until now, an instant celebrity.

Throughout history, our Constitution, the Constitution of the United States of America, has been rewritten. But if you're like me, you never thought that the Constitution would ever really change again. But we should have paid better attention in our history classes because, if we had, then we'd have known that the Constitution was built to be fluid.

Anyone hear of a little thing called the Bill of Rights, which added 10 amendments? You might not remember that the Bill of Rights was added eighteen months after the Constitution was drafted. From 1789 to 1992, the Constitution was amended 27 times!

And, through judicial review, the meaning of parts of the Constitution has been changed many times. But I bet you didn't know this: There's a magical Article that could change the Constitution completely, Article 5, which notes the concept of the Amendment Convention.

What's that, you say? Well, no one really knows. It's not been used. The power or limits of such a convention are unknown because there has never been a time in history, except for now of course, in which this article was utilized. Scholars tell me, though, that a Convention would be able to propose any change to the Constitution it decided to, including full replacement. Did you hear that? FULL REPLACEMENT! *I bet you never knew that. I sure didn't.*

So obviously, that's where we are today. That's how the former United States radically changed the Constitution and our government. That's how we ended up with President Kinji on the West and yours truly as President of the East, and states in between naturally. Some say that our great nation has been hacked, sawed in two, and destroyed. If you believe the late night talk show hosts, we've become like Oz, with witches of the East and West, and everyone waiting for Dorothy to deliver the broomstick.

But we've got to stop thinking that way! We are the same great nation under God. We are! We are merely exercising our right to tap into Article 5. We did this within the Constitution, as laid out to us by our forefathers. We are not divided! We are united in our history. We are united in our memories of an early America.

You don't believe that America has ever wanted change? We have precedent, you know. There have been many proposals for substantial change to the Constitution throughout history. Thomas Jefferson himself was wary of the power of the dead over the living, something that would happen if we had an unchanging Constitution. Without giving you too much of a history lesson, let me say this: To guarantee that each generation has a say in the framework of the government, Jefferson proposed that the Constitution, and each one following it, would expire after 19 or 20 years. Expire!

Jefferson advised that we retool, we update, we re-evaluate, we re-organize. Jefferson knew that life is about changing. America would change; and the government needed to change along with it. The people needed to have the freedom to change our government. Jefferson said this! Long before the Big War!

Let's stay in early American history for a while. In 1932, William Kay Wallace, a U.S. diplomat, proposed not only changing the Constitution, but replacing it! He would replace the states with nine geographically-based entities, each with an equal representation in a national Board of Directors. A President would be chosen from the Board; the new states would have similar systems. Sound familiar?

Back in 1932 we were talking about changing things up, governing ourselves differently; even dividing the states up into groups. What's so new about what's going on today? What's so new about the concept of two Presidents? Nothing! Turns out, it's not such a new idea after all. Someone thought of it way back in 1932.

Let's move ahead to the World War 11 era, specifically 1942. Henry Hazlitt, a conservative journalist, wrote that the time of the War was a perfect time to contemplate changing the Constitution; and that the War was pointing out several of the Constitution's weaknesses. Alexander Hehmeyer, who wrote a book in 1943, also thought that the war period was a perfect time to institute change, when people were in crisis mode. War time? Crisis mode? Sound familiar?

History repeats itself. We aren't doing anything new here! We are the <u>same</u> America! We are responding to the times, just like we've always done.

Which brings us to Thomas Finletter, a special assistant to the Secretary of State, who authored a book published in 1945: He proposed to allow the President to dissolve Congress and the Presidency. You see where I'm going with this?

We Americans have thought about shaking things up way before now. We are the creators here, the innovators, the movers and shakers. We are the Super Power. We did not crumble, we were not 'divided and conquered' as some have said. We simply pioneered a new trail; a trail that many of us have thought was a long time in coming. A trail that Jefferson envisioned from the very beginning!

Think this is all ancient history? Let's move ahead now to 1974. Rexford Tugwell, an economist who worked with FDR, *suggested we have two Vice-Presidents instead of just one. Hey, we did that! We have two Vice-Presidents. Sure, we threw in an extra President too, but you see what I'm saying. We Americans have been mulling over making changes for years! Big ones! From our forefathers up until contemporary times!*

This is not new, people. We are not brought to reform against our will. We walk willingly forward, boldly! The terrorists did not do this to us. We have the power here. We have the voice. We have the freedom to choose.

Let's move forward again in time. After Watergate, there were many calls for changes in the Constitution. That should surprise no one.

But let's skip ahead to even more contemporary times. Arthur Miller, law professor at George Washington University, wrote a book published in 1987, that called for, among other things, the redrawing of state lines. Redrawing of state lines! Re-structuring! See? We have done nothing new here. We have had these ideas in early history, and we've had them as recently as 1987.

Now we're getting close to present day, and we can't really talk about voices of reform without focusing on the Internet. Wow, do we ever have the freedom to voice who we are as Americans, and what we want. So what were people saying, in the years, months, weeks, and yes, even days before the Big War?

'The U.S. Constitution for 21st Century' web site had posted this quote: 'Unique, innovative, venerable in its time, our more than 200-year old Constitution now has become antiquated and obsolete — even detrimental and dangerous — for the nation.' Now does that sound like an America that doesn't want change? This is but a tiny sample of what the American people were saying about our Constitution right up to the day we forever changed as a nation. The day we became 'divided' as some have called it – is that the right way to look at it?

Are we 'divided'? No! If you've paid attention, and I thank you for your patience, then you know I'm leading up to this: We are still the United States of America, one nation, under God. We are. We are whole. We are together. We are one. We have restructured.

We have listened to the call for change. That's all. We are still America. And to that end: God Bless America!

John Williams gave a flourishing salute to presumably all Americans, and waited for the predictable cheers. William, who was last year a little-known but long-time senator, was now one of the most famous faces in the world, as the first President the New Conservative Party, which some had characterized as nothing more than a revamped version of the disbanded Republican Party. Conversely, the Democratic Union was often characterized as old guard Dems, even though President Kinji described herself as an Independent.

President Ann Kinji held the honor of being both the first female president, and the first Japanese-American president, of the Democratic Union. Kinji, who had been a Presidential cabinet appointee during the years leading up to World War III, was, not surprisingly, a well-known force in the then Democratic Party. The party system had been abolished post WWIII, but nonetheless, Kinji's cabinet, and all of her supporters, had been dubbed "The New Liberals". Many Americans, Paul included, believed that the two party system had never died, but lived on under new labels.

The split of the United States of America was the result of six months of emotional deliberation without a single recess, and was, in the end, swiftly agreed to with very little opposition, with no one but the media allowed in. Every American could watch history play out on their televisions, computers, phones, hand-held gadgets, and even large screens on metro buildings. But watching from afar was not good enough for Paul. Whenever he could be there in person, he was.

~~ ~~

He was in the crowd in Chicago when the last President of the United States, the *real* President, shocked the world with words that still rang in Paul's head. That famous speech, the transcript, and excerpts, now re-printed on everything from posters to blankets, was in sharp contrast to the political rhetoric he'd just heard Williams spew. No, the most famous speech in the world was full of real heartbreak, real grief, real tears. It was worthy to be listed alongside any speech of Abraham Lincoln's. It was a speech in which no one took a breath, straining to hear every incredible syllable. For generations to come, people would recall where their ancestors were when they heard this speech:

Emergency times call for emergency measures. The needs of the East and the West are diverse. We have eight U.S. governors in a perpetual state of emergency, while five states are unsafe to reside in, and three states are completely gone. This is not the time for politics or party lines. We need to remove all obstacles. This must be a working government, running not on principles and ideas, but we must instead be as foremen leading re-construction.

For the good of the country, I will step down as President of the United States, after appointing not one, but two, Presidents to govern over this beloved nation. It will take all of us working together to rewrite our Constitutional laws, and to pass all the necessary bills to make this happen, but I know we can do it. We must do it. We must come together to create a new, more efficient, way to govern. Our nation has changed.

We are a nation in crisis, unparalleled to anything the world has seen. We need an emergency response, a response that will streamline government. We will face difficulties beyond what our forefathers ever imagined. We must find a way to get closer to the people, to get smaller, to delegate the workload of rebuilding our nation.

I believe in this plan. I believe that our nation is best served by two Presidents, and by both parties, in a shared system of government that divides the nation into two equal parts. With your blessing, I will appoint two people to serve for a period of 18 months. But I assure you, elections will be held swiftly, to replace my appointees with the choice of the people.

The two Presidents shall work together, but will govern separately, much the way our individual states have always been served by Governors. This is not the death of America, but an emergency response to emergency conditions. We shall forever in our hearts be one nation under God, and though divided by governing bodies, still indivisible in spirit. With liberty and justice for all, may we one day soon be a prosperous nation once again, whose citizens live without fear, and whose children know peace. God bless America.

~~ ~~

Paul would never forget that speech, and he felt that President John Williams missed the mark entirely with his own attempt at making a speech for the history books. Williams could never match the passion or talent for oration that the former president had, even though Williams was pompous enough to try, and obviously thought of himself as an equal or, Paul sneered, even the better man. No, Williams was the inferior man in Paul's eyes, in polish, strength, and cleverness.

But when it came to honest conviction, Paul suspected that John might actually believe a little more of what he was saying, a little more. Williams was a dangerous hothead though, and Paul knew that he was better off working a different angle to get himself onto Capitol Hill, the new Capitol Hill. No matter, the doors were flung wide open for Paul, most unexpectedly. He had been waiting all his life for such an opportunity to come knocking, and here it was, an opportunity he created for himself.

From this moment on, the gap between himself and the heels of all the government insiders was shrinking. Paul, with his pretty-boy good looks, was an easy fit for the political scene. He was already well on his way to being an insider. All he needed was the right door to open, and he had found one. What he never expected was for his chosen doorkeeper to be tapped to be one of the first Presidents of the newly divided, formerly known as, United States of America.

CHAPTER 4

President Ann Kinji tucked her smooth shiny locks behind her ears. Her beautiful hair, cut in a bob, was the envy of middle class American women. Salons received many requests for what became known as "The Kinji": a smart sleek bob, which often included coloring the hair to match Kinji's onyx shade. The woman who was now an international icon was little-known prior to the Big War. It was crazy to go from obscurity to having a hair style named after her.

Beyond lack of celebrity status, Kinji's work for the previous administration, the last administration of what was once The United States of America, had done little to prepare her. Of course, how could anyone prepare to be one of the first Presidents of the nation now referred to as "The States of America"? *Everything's pretty much the same – just add a second president -- and life moves on. And if you believe that, I have some nuclear wasteland to sell you.*

Kinji snapped herself out of her brooding and studied her desk. It was tidy, that was for sure. She had so many assistants fussing over it that there wasn't a thing out of place. There were no personal items on it yet, not a single framed picture or even a coffee mug. Kinji couldn't bring herself to move in. It didn't feel real, and she wasn't sure if she was living a dream or a nightmare. She was insane if she wanted this responsibility, this crushing burden of being a pioneer in a newly divided nation. And the first female President besides? *And* Japanese? Well, the days ahead were going to be interesting.

"President Kinji?" Breyana Robertson, a strawberry blonde 20-something in a purple pants suit, rapped gently at her open door.

"Yes?" Kinji locked eyes with Breyana. It was trademark Kinji: unflinching directness that intimidated most people, but Breyana was a confident young woman and returned Kinji's gaze unwaveringly. Breyana had nothing but open admiration, respect, and hopeful aspiration to friendship.

"Paul Tracy is here to see you."

"Oh yes, send him in, please."

Paul waltzed into the room as if his steps had been choreographed, and as often as he'd played this moment in his head, they were. "President Kinji, you look so natural in this office, in front of that seal."

The Democratic Union seal depicted an eagle with an olive branch in its beak. The eagle was tinted a pale blue. The Liberty Union seal, behind President John William's desk, was identical in design, with the only difference being the color tint of the eagle, a reddish pink hue.

"Thank you, Paul. We've both put on a lot of mileage since the Warsaw days, good old Warren Academy. I hear you are going places yourself."

"It's been awhile since I've seen you. You've heard right: I've been hitting the pavement to get those bills signed. I'm proud to claim my contribution to the New Liberals."

"Democratic Union. Let's drop the polarizing label."

"Democratic Union, then."

"Is there something you want, Paul? I am due for a press conference in five minutes."

"I would like a position in your cabinet."

Kinji laughed. "Finally, somebody around here who lays it on the table."

"You know me, Ann." Paul stared into her dark eyes, leaning forward with both of his palms on her desk.

"President Kinji. Sorry, Paul, I don't do casual. No friends, no favors. If I consider this, it will be based on what you can do for my administration, period."

Paul backed away, holding his hands up. "Fair enough, Madam President. I left a package with Miss Robertson that I think will interest you. When you see what I have to offer, I'm sure I'll be hearing from you."

~~ ~~

Clyde was rugged without the handsome: oily reddish-grey hair that was sparse on top of his head, but long and stringy everywhere else; eyes set too far apart, giving him a wall-eyed look; a pitted face with a nose that snorted a long draw of mucus every few minutes.

"Morning!" he bellowed, in a deep voice that begged to be cleared of phlegm.

The sanctuary returned the greeting with a deadpan chant-like chorus of "Morning."

"You don't get Internet, and you get limited TV – just what the old rabbit ears pick up. You rely on us to keep you informed. That's why it's so important that all of you be here. Now I'll turn it over to Paul Tracy."

Paul was a man of frat-boy good looks. He was tall and lean, with thick wavy brown hair and perfect teeth – a refreshing contrast from Clyde. People were always surprised when they learned that the two men were brothers.

"Thank you for your faithfulness, and a warm welcome to the newcomers. Consider this your welcome wagon. You got your packet, and should have your new names." Paul paused while the tell-tale rustle of papers indicated that people were opening their envelopes to look.

Serena turned to Tom, "Only our last names, right? We figured that we would have to. We don't have to change our first names too, do we?"

Tom opened the packet. "They strongly suggested we change our names completely, but agreed to let us do only our last names."

"Good! What is our new last name?

"Meadows."

"Meadows?"

"You like it?"

"I guess so. Did you pick it, or did he?"

"He had a list. I thought it was the best one."

"Okay, I don't care. We'll get used to it."

"Right, that's what I thought."

"What else did he say?"

"We can't communicate with people who knew us when we were the Bridge family. I said okay, but I know we're not going to let our family and friends think we're dead forever."

"What does it matter, now that Mom is gone?"

Tom looked at her with his most sincere expression of sympathy and squeezed her hand. "She's not the only person who cared about you."

Serena didn't answer. The grief was only six months old. She was still struggling to hold herself together. Being her mother's caretaker had given her too many intimate moments with her. It would take time to heal, which was what she told herself whenever she felt like the rain would fall forever.

"As soon as things happen, we'll contact everybody, but in the meantime, I think we should do whatever the off-grid people want us to do."

"Exactly, I agree. What if we did all this and there was no reason to do it, and we're stuck in hiding because we burnt down our own house? How many laws have we broken now? I feel like such a criminal."

"I don't think anything else was illegal, just the arson."

Tom and Serena stared at each other and laughed at the absurdity, and the shock from a word like "arson" being owned by either of them.

"You should be used to it. You had to have straddled some legal lines when I met you," said Tom.

"Serena Wilcox, private detective? It's been so long since I've been that person. I'm Serena Bridges now. No, I take that back. Serena Meadows." Serena looked like she had tasted something sour.

"Maybe it's time you found her again."

"My 'mom' and 'wife' self doesn't measure up?"

"I just mean we could use a detective. We didn't learn much about this Paul guy, except that he's operating out of Minneapolis." He studied his wife's face and added, "Getting your old spunk back wouldn't hurt."

The crowd settled down and they directed their eyes obediently toward the pulpit, where Paul was gearing up for a sermon. His voice was smooth and steady, hypnotic in delivery. His eyes locked personally into each and every pair of eyes staring back at him. His audience was as captive as a warren of rabbits listening to a coyote sounding off in the distance.

They say we need the Identity Chip. What is this chip but a high-tech horror? It was the first thing I thought of when there was talk about inserting tracking chips under babies' skin so that we can solve our missing children problems. Everyone would be assigned a unique computer code – a number. You get it on the forehead or the hand. It assigns you a number, a number! Doesn't that sound familiar? Isn't that just like the Bible foretold would happen? Is this not the number of The Beast?

The chip is like a bar code. Everyone's ID will be on it, including bank routing info. No more credit cards, cash, etc. All is instant transfer. Everything digital, no need for hardcopy IDs, no more checkbooks or credit cards – just scan the forehead or back of hand. They are already doing it. Remember that story about the rich people who were too lazy to bother getting out a credit card at their favorite club, so they got a chip in their hand that the bartender scans while they sit there enjoying their drinks? Buying and selling will be through this number. Anyone read the book of Revelations? It's all right there. This is prophesy, people!

Hard to believe anyone would get the number? Think that even people who aren't religious would be a little spooked by this? Well it's also hard to believe that the government would be focusing on this chip when we've just been bombed by nuclear warheads! No one's going to want to have a tracking device inside them, but they'll do it. People will rush to do anything if they think they'll be safe. And people believe in their government.

These are like pet locator chips, but for people, so the government can track us like animals. Or, as they put it, anyone on the terrorist watch list. And missing people or criminals. They give it a good sell. How to identify bodies and missing persons is always one of the first things a government does when there is a disaster. Think of earthquakes. Special interest groups who want that chip bill passed can slide it under the radar during this emergency.

Think it sounds far-fetched? Think that the President wouldn't be getting some obscure bill passed after we just go bombed? Think again. It's happening people. You know it is. And that's why you're all here.

Senator Birmingham has urged the President to immediately sign the Identity Chip bill as an emergency measure to handle the overwhelming task of identifying missing persons. Says our senator, 'While the measure will not aid in the recovery efforts now underway, the measure could benefit any future national crises."

Think, people. The 'Beast' from the Bible is a computer, not a person. The chip, the number, will soon be the only way to pay for things, and it tracks every purchase you make. That's how they can keep track of people buying things that are a red flag for terrorism and other criminal intentions, and it's how they can track you! Us!

Economists say there will be no more problems with insufficient funds – important when the economy falls out. It all sounds logical, logical enough that a lot of people will line up voluntarily to get the chip. I am thinking that after today, it will be like the McCarthy era, and everyone will be paranoid about who everyone is. Our citizenship and other basic info, arrest record, anything, can be added to that chip. People will want this. They will think that they are protecting themselves.

And I mention 'the President' so casually. We are under the regime of not one, but two presidents, who want this chip. If you disagree with President John Williams and hope to jump a couple states over to the West to live under President Kinji, whatever farce her liberal administration is, well, you've got a rude awakening. They both want the chip. In fact, she wants it more than Williams does. This chip is the beginning of communism.

The weight of hearing Paul's right-winged speech of paranoid delusion was starting to press down upon them and both were suddenly very tired, so very tired. What was the most fatiguing of all was the fact that Tom and Serena shared this man's delusion. For it was the fear of getting this Identity Chip, this fear most of all of allowing such a chip to be inserted into their precious children, was the catalyst for their fiery exodus from life as normal upstanding citizens and into this land of crazy people. But these were crazy times.

During the next break between speeches, Serena said to Tom, "Five years since the bombings. And it's been two since the restructuring. I still can't get used to Chicago being the nation's capital. And with Minneapolis the new 'wall street', it's like the whole country has moved over to the left."

"The left?"

"To the left of the map, like if you were looking at it."

"You mean 'West'?"

"Okay, then, West."

"And East – we are moved in on both sides."

"With California gone, we have Denver as the 'new Hollywood'. It's hard to believe all of this has happened. Just a few years ago, life was normal, despite recessionary times."

"It's surprising so few actors died. Not too many were in California when they got hit."

"Makes you wonder if the rich and famous got a heads-up that the rest of the population didn't."

"It's possible."

"Our government knew. Politicians were out of D.C. and government buildings and military installations were evacuated."

"Nothing's been proven about that," Tom cautioned. He feared that they were becoming as crazy as the off-grid people.

"No, but it's not like we can't figure it out. How else did so many people get out in time? We didn't lose any senators, and no Generals."

"True."

"It's hard to accept that a senator's life is worth more than an ordinary American citizen's. How can that be right? Millions died, while the political people and the celebrities got a heads-up and lived."

"*We* lived," Tom reminded her.

Serena was quiet for a few seconds. "But we were lucky -- blessed. Why couldn't the government warn people? They would have had hard intelligence from satellites or something. Were they afraid of mass panic and then no one could get out?"

"Maybe. I saw a new map at the library. It was sad seeing the United States smaller, and divided. California, Virginia, Pennsylvania and part of New York were grayed out. Oregon, New Jersey and part of Michigan were filled in with a dot pattern for 'uninhabitable'."

"And now we are split in two, with two presidents. Nothing feels real anymore."

The break was over and Paul had returned to the pulpit. He took a sip of bottled water and revved himself up into his closing rant.

People, listen. It's coming fast. They are putting chips in all new babies born on or after January 1. In three weeks. And by April 1, every citizen is required to have the chip. They are already putting the chips in prisoners and anyone who comes in to renew a driver's license.

Cameras they have now can scan license plates and alert the police if there's anything going on with your vehicle – unpaid parking tickets, crime committed, or stolen vehicle. We've had this awhile. But now they'll be using it to catch those who don't have the chip.

We at OGG, off-grid-ghost, we are officially urging people to get the chips.

Paul waited for his words to register with the crowd. He was not disappointed by their reaction of gasps, followed by shocked silence.

Seriously, we do. It's the only way to protect ourselves. We get the chip, and then come in to OGG. We'll set you up with a code that we'll add to the chip that blocks the data. It is like a virus blocker, like a firewall for when you're on the Internet and someone's trying to steal your identity. When anyone scans the chip, it will give them limited data: whatever the off-grid programmers put in. It won't track your real transactions. But it will protect you. It will satisfy the government that you have the chip.

And we control the number, so that no one here ends up with 666 embedded under their skin.

Paul laughed, and the audience responded in kind. Tom and Serena exchanged looks of horror, not mirth.

Paul continued.

I'm not sure that the Beast is a computer, or that the numbers are about the Identity Chip. But do we want to take a chance? Of course we don't! The Identity Chip is required to get a driver's license, and banks will use it for all transactions. Stores will use it for all transactions. What will we do for money? How will we get around? If you don't have the chip, you can be arrested.

Let us help you. What we are offering you is software to add to the chip, our mark. The software is called "Angels Mark", and we strongly suggest you get the chip, come directly to OGG, and get Angels Mark installed. Do this by April 1. It gives you three months. We want all of our members protected by then. And from that point onward, only those with the Angels Mark will be able to scan to get into the OGG campus. We are doing this for all of us. Outsiders will find us eventually, but we don't want to make it easy for them to get in. So get the chip. Then come to us. We'll help you hide. We'll protect you.

Paul ended his final speech with a confident nod to the crowd. They responded with strong applause and a few scattered Amens. Everyone quickly dispersed, with many making a beeline toward Paul and his staff. Tom and Serena dodged the beaten path and bolted for the nearest exit.

Serena barely waited until the van door was shut behind her before saying, "They won't know we don't have the Angels Mark unless we try to get on the off-grid campus. If we use these three months to stock up on food and supplies, we could stay here for a lot longer than three months without anyone knowing we don't have it."

"We stock up. After April 1, we stop going to the off-grid campus."

"How long can we live without going to the store? We won't be able to go shopping anywhere."

"We can get chickens."

"We'd need a chicken coop."

"I can build one."

"We can grow our own food. This is going to be an adventure."

"It will be fun, besides, what choice do we have?"

CHAPTER 5

Paul Tracy left the seminar feeling as if he'd just sold his last vacuum cleaner of the day, in other words: victorious and vindicated. Funny how those old feelings resurfaced after so many years. It seemed like another lifetime ago that Paul had been a vacuum cleaner salesman, a job for which he had a natural gift. He outsold everyone, despite never getting a good client list. Most of his sales went to people who couldn't afford them, and virtually all of his sales went to people who had no intention of buying a vacuum cleaner that day, not until Paul showed up on their door step.

He was initially motivated to hard-sell to impress his boss, to prove that he was not too young to hold down a job, but Paul was quickly bitten by the bug; he craved the gambler's high that selling gave him. The rush, lasting for a few glorious moments, sometimes hours, was what drove him toward making the next sale. He became a master at conning homeowners and renters alike with his slick tricks to demonstrate how dirty their floors were from using their current sweeper, and then dazzling them with how clean the new sweeper got their floors.

Paul polished off his act until he had a fail-proof, show-stopping, demonstration and a one-in-three sales track record. Not bad for a kid fresh out of high school. Eventually, the job he viewed as a perfectly-legal con game was effortless. Paul was Salesman of the Month every month without fail, for the entire four years he worked for Morris Handley.

Morris was a weasel of a man. He even looked like a weasel: He had a slight build that couldn't accommodate his extra pounds, giving him a small-animal-with-a-pouchy-belly physique. Add his oval head with wide-set eyes and pointy ears, and it wasn't hard to imagine him as anthropomorphic vermin.

Paul, who enjoyed his own reflection in the mirror, noticed all of Morris' shortcomings, especially the receding hairline that was poorly, and absurdly, masked by a cosmetic spray that looked suspiciously like black spray paint. And if the physical appearance wasn't eye candy enough, Morris gave something special to the ears as well. He had a voice that defied explanation. It was both nasal and a low baritone; it was both gritty and strong. The rise in pitch went up two octaves when he was yelling at his salesmen, but would fall sharply and unexpectedly into the throaty bear growl of a mobster.

Saving the best attribute for last, Morris had an overbearing wife who called the office incessantly with her constant carping. When Morris was especially beleaguered by the steady barrage of nagging and barbs from his wife, he would vent his pent-up frustrations at Paul and the other young salesmen. All of the young men, and one unfortunate young lady who was perpetually the victim of sexual harassment by pretty much everyone (she only lasted two months at Handley Sweep & Repair), were reduced to putty when Morris bellowed, all but Paul.

Paul always took the abuse cheerfully and then set out to out-sell everyone else. Before long, he was the apple of Morris' eye. Day after day, Paul set out with his vacuum kit until that fateful day that he landed at the front door of Miss Donna. Miss Donna was known in the area, and avoided. But Paul had never heard of her, or her conquests, of which there had been many.

Miss Donna, home all day without a job, was leery of a stranger showing up unannounced, but after looking Paul over, she ushered him inside. She was lonely with the kids all grown up all off to their fancy schools. Why they needed college, she'd never understand. Her kids would be in debt for the rest of the lives and for what? Did they think they were too good for a real job? Didn't her daughter get it by now, that husbands leave or die? Why bother with more school when it won't pay the rent? Don't get her started on her son, he was a closed subject. And if the subject was opened, well, Donna had a lot to say.

Then along came Paul, who was the same age as Miss Donna's own son. Paul was good looking, better looking than her son. Paul looked like he played sports and his skin was tan from sun – not like her son, who was pasty white and couldn't catch a ball. Her son would rather stay inside and read a book all summer than join the team. Paul had a real job. She admired Paul's full head of hair. He looked so young and virile. Before she was fully aware of what she was doing, Miss Donna had reached out to touch Paul's hair.

Paul flinched, but he didn't pull away. He only stood there, blinking his eyes in surprise. He let his box of supplies slip to the floor, making a soft thump on the carpet. Miss Donna's cool blue eyes sized him up in an instant and she lunged at him, clutching both sides of his face with her dry thin hands and long stained fingernails. She pressed her lips onto his, so hard that Paul felt pain. She wriggled her tiny body like a hairless cat while working with her lips to open Paul's unresponsive mouth.

Paul was slow to react, but his brain finally spoke to his hands. He pushed Miss Donna away with more force than he intended. She looked at him with wide eyes and an open mouth: horror. Then her eyes and mouth relaxed into a mask of tragedy: humiliation. Last, her eyes narrowed into catlike slits and fixed on him with a vengeance: hatred. Paul knew those three H's well: horror, humiliation, and hatred. He'd seen them before, and he knew he was in trouble.

By the time he reached Handley Sweep & Repair, he had rehearsed his story dozens of times. It would be her word against his, and he guessed, correctly, that she had picked up the phone the moment he walked out the door. She would make a complaint about Paul before he could make a complaint about her, of that he was certain. The question was, who did she call? Did she ring Morris, or had she gone straight to the police?

Much to Paul's relief, the complaint had been made to Morris only, no police. But Morris was irate. All of the repressed anger he felt day after day in his shabby little life with his carpy wife boiled over. He let loose like a short fat bull throwing a tantrum. Paul was reminded of a cartoon character, the Disney-fied Danny DeVito in Hercules. He almost started laughing, almost.

"What did you think you were doing!"

"Sir, I didn't do anything wrong."

"I know you didn't!"

"I don't know what she told you, but I didn't do anything."

"I should fire you right now."

"But you won't." Paul said calmly. *Cool as a cucumber*, he coached himself. He knew he was the best that Morris had, and Morris wouldn't let him go based on one complaint from Miss Donna. He tried to push the image of the animated Danny DeVito character out of his head.

"You are my best salesman, but don't think I won't fire you if you don't make this right."

"I'll be on guard in the future."

"What? No you won't. You'll go right back to Donna's and make sure she's a satisfied customer."

Paul blinked hard, finally catching on to what Morris was saying. "What do you mean, sir? She didn't order anything."

"You know what I mean. Donna only complains when she doesn't get what she wants. You're young, you're her type. Don't think I don't know what happened."

"Nothing happened."

"Yeah. Make sure that something does."

"You can't be serious."

Morris came out from behind his metal desk, a desk littered with children's school pictures, office supplies and paperwork that Morris should have completed weeks ago. A pizza box with one piece left in it topped the stack. His body brushed the pile, causing the tower to slide off the desk. Morris seemed not to notice.

He walked toward Paul until he was standing only a few inches from his face. Morris, several inches shorter than Paul, had somehow made himself tall enough to look him eye to eye. He reached out and gripped Paul's shoulders with his hairy stubby fingers.

"Look kid, it's a tough world. I'm doing you a favor. You have something that women want." His halitosis expelled over Paul's face like an exterminator's fogger. He growled, "A pretty boy like you. Use it."

Paul left Handley Sweep & Repair and went directly home, to the empty house that had once been occupied a happy family. Well, to be fair, the family was never all that happy, but at least they were together, all of them alive. Imperfect parents were nearly always better than dead parents. They'd been gone a long time now and Paul had trouble remembering what it was like to have had parents; his brother Clyde had been his legal guardian since Paul was thirteen years old.

The empty house seemed to echo his every step, mocking him. Paul was aching for his parents even though he knew deep down that he probably wouldn't have shared any of this Miss Donna situation with them. It was a relief when a clatter from the kitchen caught Paul's ears: Clyde was home.

"Why are you home?" Paul asked.

Clyde didn't pause in his dish-washing routine. "I could ask the same of you, little brother."

"I'm in trouble, Clyde."

"Oh?" Clyde dried his hands on the faded green-checked dish towel hanging from the front pocket of his jeans. He turned away from the sink.

"This nasty old bat came on to me and I got out of there. Morris wants me to go back to her and do what she wants."

"Mole-man? He's pulling your leg."

"No, he's serious. And it's a gopher. He looks like a gopher."

"Mole, gopher – a rodent is a rodent. How do you know he's not messing with your head?"

"He wants the sale. He's not joking."

"You're telling me that the scumbag would pimp out my little brother to sell a vacuum cleaner?"

"If you don't believe me, listen to this." Paul fished his cell phone out of his pocket.

"You recorded him?"

"Audio. There's no video, I kept it in my pocket."

"I'm impressed."

Clyde listened to Morris' tirade, and could hear for himself the unmistakable meaning of what Morris told Paul to do. Clyde felt the blood rushing to his head, his hands clenched into fists. He willed his body to relax. He tensed his face and then released the tension. He took a couple deep breaths. When he had stabled himself he said, "I'll take care of it. You go on to the rest of your route. Say nothing about Donna."

"How did you know it was her?"

Clyde held up the clipboard Paul had set on the kitchen table. "You checked off all the names before hers. Besides, she has a reputation. Figured she was the one."

"You got it right. It's her." Paul shuddered at the memory of her moist hot lips on his mouth.

"Don't worry, kid. I've got your back. You check off her name. Mark it as 'not home'. Go to the next person on your list. Business as usual. Say nothing to Morris, or anyone. Got it?"

Paul opened his mouth to ask what Clyde was going to do, but something in his brother's face stopped him cold. Paul left the kitchen, went upstairs to his room, and spent the rest of his Friday afternoon listening to music. By Sunday, Paul had two nights of hard partying with his friends behind him and had almost forgotten about Miss Donna.

The following Monday morning, when Paul arrived early, without a trace of a hangover, Morris pulled Paul into his office for a chat. "Paulie, I got something to tell you."

What was that expression on Morris' face? Compassion? Pity? Were rodents capable of emotion? Paul waited, said nothing.

"It's about Donna. Drop her from your list. She's dead. Her son found her body on Saturday. It was a freak accident. Somehow she fell into her bathtub full of water – her clothes still on and everything. Her blow dryer was plugged in nearby, it was in the tub – switch was on. They think she might have grabbed at the cord as she was falling, or was stupid enough to dry her hair while in the tub. I don't know if she died from hitting her head on the tub, from zapping herself, or from drowning. Whatever. She's dead. Take her off your roster."

Paul blinked. He said nothing. His mind fleetingly went to Clyde. Could Clyde have had something to do with Donna's death? No, of course not! "Are the police investigating?"

Morris snorted. "I doubt it. What's one less skank in this town?"

Paul continued selling vacuum cleaners for another six long months, until he had enough money in his bank account to make a down payment on a small business loan. After that, Paul would never have to sell another vacuum. Because, according to Clyde, there was a little something that Morris was completely clueless about: who owned the building, the hole-in-the-wall hovel in a God-forsaken town, where Handley Sweep & Repair had been in business for three generations. Clyde knew, and he filled Paul's head with a plan to get out from under Morris Handley with his middle finger held high.

The history on the Handley building involved the late Mr. Ferro, a dear friend of Morris' grandfather, who helped the Handley family in the early days when Mr.

Handley was supporting an ill wife and a young family with eleven children. Ferro set a lower-than-market-price rental agreement, something Mr. Handley could afford to pay – and yet maintain his pride in supporting his family.

In over forty years, Ferro had never raised the rent, even when Handley Sweep & Repair was passed down through two generations. When Ferro's daughter Martha inherited the Handley Sweep & Repair building from her father, she had no interest in the building and made no changes to the original rental agreement that her father had with Morris. She had never visited the building, probably never read the rental agreement, and Clyde suspected that she would rather get rid of it than continue the relationship with the Handleys; who, two generations removed from the original Ferro-Handley friendship, were strangers to each other, and not in the same league as Martha and her circle.

Paul made Martha an offer for the building. She didn't hesitate to sell it to the promising young man, so enterprising and energetic. Making something new out of something neglected? Her father would have appreciated such idealism and work ethic. How wonderful to be out from under the Handley building with a sale she could feel good about. Secretly, Martha was, above everything else, pleased that she no longer had any association with the Handleys, which was precisely what Clyde expected.

What Clyde also knew was that Morris was in debt, a deep dark abyss of debt that Morris would never be able to repay, even if he worked hard for the rest of his life. His shrew of a wife had overextended their credit cards, again, and the Handleys were in serious danger of losing their house. The poor chump couldn't even declare personal bankruptcy because he had already done that all too recently. There was no more recourse for Morris and Clyde knew that Morris would not be able to hold on to Handley Sweep & Repair if the rent was, say, triple what he was currently paying.

As per Clyde's instruction, Paul promptly changed the rental agreement. The original contract had long expired and had no legal standing, so there was no barrier in the way of immediately raising the rent to what the current market would bear. Eventually Morris would fall so far behind in payments that eviction would be the next step.

During the planning stage, Paul had asked, "But why bother with any of this? I can just quit Handley's and get a different job."

Clyde scowled, "Paul, you can't let him run you off. You have to take back your power."

"You've been watching too much daytime TV," Paul scoffed.

Clyde didn't crack a smile. "This isn't something to play around with. You let this rodent squeeze you out, and you'll be under someone's feet the rest of your life. There will be another Morris right behind this one."

"Why don't I just kick him out right away? Why wait months?"

"Patience, little brother. Watch him squirm. Revenge is sweeter when it takes time to unfold. And when it does, you can throw away your cheap polyester suit."

After three years of selling vacuums, Paul was done with that forever. And Clyde was right; it was a sweet victory to watch Morris beg for extensions when the rent came due each month. Paul stretched out the enjoyment by allowing extensions, with interest, for over six months. Then Paul sent Morris' account to collections. Finally, nine months after Paul had purchased the Handley Sweep & Repair building, he evicted Morris.

Paul, at twenty-one years of age, knew that his revenge marked the last time he would ever answer to anyone. But after his revenge on Morris was complete, he was stuck with Morris' old haunt. What to do with it? Lease it, sell it or use it? He turned the matter over to Clyde.

Clyde needed no arm twisting. He was waiting for Paul to finally realize that something would need to be done about the building now that it was vacant. He offered, helpfully, to partner with Paul, and he was quick to spin the situation until his younger brother believed that Clyde would respect Paul as an equal, or even, laughably, as a senior. It amused Clyde that Paul was so easily manipulated that Paul was actually seeking him out for help, without a clue that Clyde had been "helping" him all along. Clyde cursed the fact that Paul was not a twin, and was not even a full brother, but Paul was as close as Clyde would get to an alter ego. Messing with Paul's head was child's play; he was a soft lump of clay that was no challenge for a skilled potter. After all, the conditions were ideal: Paul was a vain conventionally-handsome boy who had been flattered from birth. He would never believe that anyone could hate him or want to do him harm.

Yes, Clyde would go into business with Paul. He would be a silent *senior* partner: secretly spinning webs and twisting Paul's thoughts until Paul himself believed that Clyde's ideas were his own. That's how it had always been, and how it would always be. As for this latest development, Paul didn't come up with the Handley takeover. Of course it was Clyde who had filled his head with ideas, so naturally Clyde thought of the building as his own from the start. If Paul hadn't come to Clyde with the partnership idea on his own accord, Clyde would have spun a web to draw him to what he wanted, but Paul made things easy for Clyde, as he always did.

The two brothers agreed to hold their first business meeting at their parents' kitchen table. Catsup, two plates, two mugs, two forks, and two paper napkins were already on the table before Paul came downstairs. The smell of cooking oil greeted Paul when he entered the kitchen, reminding him that he was hungry. Without a word, Paul sat in his regular chair while Clyde fried the sliced baby red potatoes he had boiled the day before. A few moments later Clyde served up the potatoes and the coffee. Then he sat down opposite Paul.

"The old Handley building has real potential," Clyde began.

"I handled that slick, didn't I? I have to make money fast though. I burned through all my savings on the down payment." Paul drizzled catsup over his potatoes. Fried potatoes like Mom used to make, Paul's favorite.

"You don't have much time to find a new job." Clyde's eyes were full of concern. Clyde had practiced that particular expression in the mirror until he could do it on command. He could have been an actor in another life, a character actor though – he was not good looking enough to be a leading man. Paul would be the man for that job. Clyde broke free of his own musings and realized that Paul was talking. How amusing, little brother was defensive.

"I don't want a new job. I want to be my own boss," Paul bristled. Paul was amazed sometimes at how little Clyde understood him.

"You don't have time to grow a business." Clyde took a bite of potato and slowly moved his eyes in thoughtful contemplation.

"What are you saying? Go into business or not? I need money now, but I want to do this. What should I do, Clyde?"

"Too bad people wouldn't just give you money, tossing dollars into an offering plate just to see you talk."

"I could be a preacher," Paul snorted.

"Now that's an idea worth considering! The old Handley building is in an excellent location for a church. The people will pack the pews. Magnificent!" Clyde jumped up from his chair and began clearing the dishes. Every movement he made was with great gusto: Stack the plates with a clatter, clatter. Scrape, scrape the scraps into the bin. Slip it all into the sink with a satisfying plunk into the soapy water.

"I turn it into a church? You're not serious." Paul twisted his body in his chair to follow Clyde's movements as he whirled about the kitchen.

Clyde sat back down. "Sure! Start up a new church. People will pay just to hear you speak."

"I don't know, you think so?" asked Paul.

He leaned forward on the table and hid a snide grin behind pious folded hands. Paul was warming up to the idea, his ego responding to the idea of people hanging on his every word. Soft clay was never a challenge for a skilled potter like Clyde.

CHAPTER 6

President Ann Kinji typed the word "Cologne" into the online shopping search engine textbox. She was relieved to find only a dozen choices. She ignored Old Spice, which conjured up a fond memory of her grandfather, and anything that sounded like a teenage boy's scent. That left her with only two options. Of the two, she chose the best looking bottle, the one with the best reviews. *There, done!*

She knew it wasn't the most personal way to shop, but she was proud that at least she was doing her own shopping for her husband instead of delegating the task to one of her assistants. Ann had a perfect record of never missing their special occasions, regardless of how busy she was. It didn't matter if she was an overloaded college student or one of the first two Presidents of the formally-known-as United States, she had always found the time for her best friend. However, with Ted's birthday not quite two weeks away, it was too close for comfort. At least that was how it felt to Ann, who was always light years ahead of schedule. It was a telling sign that she was dangerously close to being sucked into the office; her former life a shadow.

Ann was determined to hold on to the person that she was, but that noble intention was proving more difficult than she could have imagined. The presidency had blindsided her and she was feeling unsure of herself for the first time in her life. How does one go from normal person to President? Never in her wildest dreams had she held such extreme ambition, or even the slightest expectation that a woman would become President in her lifetime, let alone an Asian woman, let alone herself!

Ann wasn't ungrateful. Her awareness of her unique place in history, her extraordinary influence in this unprecedented time of turbulence, and her power to alter fate for a nation, no, the *world*, was acute. And yet, she didn't ask for this unquantifiable responsibility. In her spirit, Ann was still that little girl sitting in the front of the class; assigned to the power seat by one teacher after another, never seeking attention for herself, but attracting it anyway. The only thing that Ann set her sights on was the pursuit of excellence in everything she did. The awards, the accolades, the acclaim – all of these were the cherry on top. Intrinsic rewards were always enough to keep her going.

Naturally, she was a teacher's dream: smart as a whip, creative, and talented, without a hint of arrogance. She was a model citizen, popular with her peers without ever joining the "in" crowd, or wasting much energy on worrying about what other people thought of her. She just did the right thing in every situation, and she worked very, very hard – joyfully; she was a ball of light. She moved as if she had the energy of the sun fueling her on, her steps as light and effortless as a flower fairy dancing in the morning light.

It was that way for Ann from birth. She was blessed to always be at the right place, at the right time, for each golden opportunity. So it was without effort that she found herself wearing a virtual crown, despite never playing political games and never compromising her moral code, not once in her twenty years of public service, not ever.

Ann was a living example of "work meets opportunity", an anomaly in politics; someone who had no connections, no family money, and not a devious bone in her body. No, she was just a very smart girl who worked her way up, up, up, -- up and out of her hometown of Warsaw, Indiana -- until one day important people tapped her to solve the world's worst problems in modern day history.

Her run-in with Paul had conjured up memories of Warsaw; walking after school to the library, waiting for her father to pick her up after work; going to Pizza King after a basketball game and giving her best friend a kick under the table to signal it was time to get away from her annoying date; buying a new dress to wear to the Snowball; feeling left out when kids told stories of cow-tipping and barn parties, even though she didn't really want to be the kind of girl who got invited to the secret parties where alcohol, and other things, flowed freely; riding with her boyfriend through the corn fields; swimming at Winona Lake and getting stuck in the seaweed.

Her mind rested on the Winona Lake story for a few minutes. When she had shouted for help, her father told her to relax, don't panic, relax. She did, and the seaweed fell away, drifting around her in a swirl of harmless green gunk. She easily swam back to the pier. *Life is like swimming in seaweed,* she mused.

She was a long way from Warsaw, where basketball was not a mere game or sport, but something as revered as a church service. She had never quite understood the love of basketball, nor did she ever really become a Hoosier – her family moved to Warsaw the summer before she entered fourth grade – but she grew up well there. Watching "brat pack" movies with her friends, attending both proms, tying for first place in the high school talent show, making the honor roll, even taking special classes for "gifted and talented".

Yes, she was still that girl, the charmed fairy princess, but her ball of light was fast dimming. She couldn't remember the last time she had really looked at her face in the mirror, beyond the face to the spirit within. She saw only what she needed to see to pull herself together each day; the blemishes to conceal, the curve of her lips to paint, the uneven complexion to smooth, the new lines on her face to mask.

In her reflection, her dark eyes stared back at her, awaiting the insertion of contact lenses and the framing of her lids with makeup, but there was no gleam, no spark of life, no glimpse of her soul. She was being eclipsed by the office she held. At what point would she disappear altogether?

Ann sensed that her husband could feel her slipping away. She hoped that her thoughtfulness on his birthday would reassure him, and she was confident that it would, for now. Ted was an easy man to please. He appreciated the simple things in life. He was also a patient man. Yet Ann knew that no marriage was immune from strain, growing apart, and ultimately ending. How long could Ted wait for intimacy to return? What was his breaking point?

Ann's moments of brooding were fleeting, but in recent days had become much more frequent, and more regretful and wistful in nature. A reoccurring theme was her longing to be a mother, which always resolved itself with the reluctant thought that her inability to conceive a child was a blessing in disguise. If she was struggling to hold on to her own identity, could she have nurtured a child?

No, she answered herself, the office consumed her; she could not have put a child first. Not only did she not have time for a theoretical child, she knew that if she didn't figure out how to get a grip on herself, she could lose her marriage by the time this was all over. But of course, maybe her destiny included making such personal sacrifices for the greater good. When put into that framework, how could she not rise to the occasion, regardless of the toll?

"President Kinji?"

"Yes?"

Breyana Robertson, in a magenta pants suit today, rapped gently at her open door, as was her ritual. “Paul Tracy is back.”

“You’ve got to be kidding me.” Ann’s shiny bob waggled, giving away the angry shaking of her head.

“Sorry. I could tell him you’re not available?” Breyana suggested, all the while knowing that Kinji would never back down from a challenge.

“No, send him in please.”

Paul strolled in front of the Democratic Union seal, looking smug and mysterious. “How are you and the New Liberals getting on?”

“Democratic Union. Get to your point.”

“Harsh, especially after what I offered you.”

“I don’t know anything about an offer, and I don’t see any reason to talk to you. I allowed you in here for the sole purpose of telling you face to face that I don’t want you to contact me again.”

“You didn’t get my package?”

“I disposed of it without opening it. I do not appease bullies.”

"That's how you see me? A bully? Why, Ann, I'm offended."

"Look, Paul, I am not a game player. I do not have any skeletons. There is nothing to blackmail me with. You have no bargaining tools. I'm asking, no, *telling*, you to leave."

"You should have opened the package, but that's okay. I have copies. You'll want to see what I have to offer."

Ann picked up the phone, but Paul flipped the stack of papers around before she could punch anything in. And the face she saw gave her pause: It was Ted. *Her* Ted. With a little girl. Walking hand-in-hand. Clearly, obviously, this child had a bond with Ted. Clearly, obviously, Ted was likely her father. Clearly, obviously, Ann did not know this child existed, nor did the rest of the world.

"I'm offering you my silence, in exchange for a job."

"I don't give in to terrorists. Not even when my personal life is at stake."

"Oh I know you don't. But you won't stand on principle at the expense of a little girl's life – think of how that child will be exploited if you let my people go public with this. I know you'll think this through, and then you'll call me. And when you do, you'll accept my offer."

He set the stack of photos on Ann's desk. As he turned around to leave, he said, "Looking forward to working with you, Ann."

"Get out."

"You'll call me. I'll give you 24 hours." And on that note, Paul spun sharply on the heels of his $700 shoes and left the office of the President of the Democratic Union, with Ann's dark eyes burning holes into his suited back.

Paul worked his way through the maze of the building, leaving the marbled-floor hallways far behind him. Fifteen minutes later, he was finally in the parking garage and searching for his beloved Porsche Carrera GT, a supercar with a top speed of 205 mph+; and, as he'd tested the claim for himself, he told anyone who would listen that it could reach 0-60 in 3.9 seconds. He'd spent $428,000 on the car, a bargain.

The economic downturn brought about opportunity for the newly rich like Paul. He loved his silver baby, and hated leaving it unprotected in a common parking garage. That was why he parked it as far away from the entrance as possible, where he was the most likely to be able to take two parking spaces for himself, a move that he regretted today.

He was all alone, on the far opposite of the highest parking ramp exit, where no one could hear him if he screamed – a thought that occurred to him when a large beefy hand grabbed his mouth shut from behind his head.

Paul tried to twist his head to see the man who held him captive, but he felt such strong resistance that he feared his neck would break if he dared try that move again. He advised himself not to resist his captor, and to wait for his chance to run.

He spied his Porsche just yards away. The sight of his car gave birth to anger, more anger than fear. Paul bit the beefy hand.

"Sonnofa…" bellowed the six foot six man, who released Paul instantly.

"Grab him," yelled another.

"Where do you think you're going?" said a third.

For the first time, Paul understood that he was grabbed by official thugs, not a mugger. Secret Service it looked like. So Ann had made good on her threat then? She was really going to toss her husband's illegitimate love child to the wolves? Heartless shrew! Paul had underestimated Kinji. And yet Clyde had been so sure that Ann would crumble.

"Sweet ride. I'll drive," said the possessor of the beefy hand.

Startled, Paul gulped, "No you won't!"

"You bit me. I drive." The giant stepped into the car and glared at Paul. "Keys."

"Get in," the second man growled as he pushed Paul closer to the passenger's door.

Beefy Hand drove Paul in the Porsche while the other two men followed in a black sedan with government plates. They traveled through heavy commuter traffic, sometimes at a stop-and-go pace, without exchanging a word. Paul tried to initiate conversation, but his attempts were answered with a silent glare. Not that he could see the man's eyes behind the dark glasses, but he could feel them. An hour and forty-five minutes later, they arrived at a private airport where a small jet awaited them.

Beefy Hand snatched Paul's coat jacket and yanked him around like he was a marionette. He propelled Paul up the narrow metal steps to the jet's open door. Once Paul was inside the plane, Beefy Hand released him and turned outward to face the tarmac. He stood guard. Against what?

Paul blinked his eyes to adjust to the difference in lighting, and walked slowly down the small aisle of, what he now recognized to be, a luxury jet. And there, two feet in front of him, sitting in a leather chair, sipping coffee, was none other than President John Williams. Paul stopped in his tracks. He feared his mouth had fallen open.

"Take a seat, Paul."

The leather chairs were positioned to face each other. There were two chairs on each side. Paul sat directly opposite the President, as that was the chair that President Williams was gesturing toward. Paul's mind was racing. Had he done anything to flag himself as a potential terrorist? What could the President want with him?

"Nice work today."

"Sir?"

"That's Mr. President."

"Sorry. Mr. President, I don't know what you are referring to. How do you know me?"

"We have ears in Kinji's office."

"You're bugging the President's office?"

"Oh don't look so surprised. You've been getting your hands dirty your own self."

"You know about that?"

"The pictures of her husband with the child. How did you do it?"

"What do you mean?"

President Williams arched an eyebrow. "Don't play stupid with me. That kid isn't his. She doesn't even exist. How did you manage to airbrush a kid who looks the spitting image of him? I want the name of your guy."

"Okay, you got me." Paul shrugged. "I don't know who did it. I have a team that works for me. They took a photo and morphed it, changed her features to look more like his. I hear it wasn't that hard to do. He has an easy face to copy."

"It's good work. I want to use it."

"Excuse me?"

"There's nothing wrong with your hearing. I want to use it, you. You're going to work for me now."

"No one owns me."

"Think again. I've caught you in this pathetic scheme of yours. What is it you were planning to do, anyway? Did you really think she would hire you if you blackmailed her? That was never going to happen."

"I know her better than you think."

"Oh, old school chums. Yes, I heard. Although I'm curious, why did you call it an Academy? My people tell me that your only childhood connection to Kinji is a babysitter in common. A Mrs. Mason, who we'd have talked to, but she's deceased. Died from a freak accident in the home."

Paul's eyes registered the shock he felt.

"You didn't know she was dead? What's it to you? Answer me about the Academy bit."

"We ran into each other when we were about sixteen or so. We made a joke about the old Academy days, Mrs. Mason headmaster. It was sarcasm. Warren Academy is a mobile home with nicotine-stained walls and mildewed furniture. We hated that place, and the nasty slug who ruled it; watching soaps all day, giving us nothing but animal crackers to eat and Kool-Aid to drink, telling us to shut up while puffing away on one cigarette after another."

A familiar face appeared at that moment. It was the blonde aide from the tarmac. Paul always remembered another good-looking man. The aide produced coffee for the President; no offer was extended to Paul. The aide sat next to John and remained there for the duration of the conversation, which Paul found curious and off-putting. Now he had two sets of eyes starting him down.

"And that's your only connection to Kinji?"

"Yes."

"She came from humble beginnings, so did you."

"What's your point?"

"No point. Forming a picture. Tell me why you wanted her to hire you."

"I can't tell you that."

"Son, I have no time for this. I have to meet Kinji myself in less than two hours. My staff can dig around and figure this out. If you make me wait for that I won't be in a generous mood anymore."

"Generous?"

"I want to hire you, Paul."

"I don't understand."

"Tell me what I need to know. Then I'll tell you what you need to know."

"I wanted to work for her so that I could influence that Identity Chip bill. I want it to pass."

"Ah, now I get it. You want fear mongering to bring more money into your church, your pocket in other words. You and your homely brother Cliff."

"Clyde."

John Williams waved his hand to indicate that Clyde's name was irrelevant to him. "Your plan was, and is, ridiculous. But your blackmail photo is quite good. I hope you are paying those kids you've got running your computer lab. It's not child slavery is it? You got them working in your cult for food and water?"

Paul's eyes again registered surprise.

"Oh you didn't think I knew all about your operation? Paul, my guys briefed me about your whole life in about fifteen minutes. It's all right here." He tapped the brown folder he held on his lap. "They said I could read it on one of them gadgets, but I like paper."

Paul knew he was beaten, in way over his head. He was nothing but a two-bit con man compared to the President of the Liberty Union. "What do you want with me?"

"I want you to take that photo of yours to the media."

"You want to embarrass her?"

"You don't need to know my reasons. But yes. Making trouble for her keeps her off balance."

"I can't believe we're having this conversation."

John snorted. "You ain't no Boy Scout, Paul. You know politics can be messy."

"Why didn't you send one of your people to talk to me? Why is the President himself doing this?"

"You're an oily little snake, Paul. You wouldn't be loyal to a staffer. But you'll be loyal to me, won't you?" The President leaned forward and locked his steely blue-gray eyes with Paul's. Satisfied, he relaxed his posture. "See? We understand each other."

"That's all you want me to do, leak the photo?"

"No. That's not all."

"Then what? And what about hiring me?"

John chuckled. "Someone will pay you. You'll find money in your account. Untraceable to this office, of course."

"And what do I have to do?"

"Leak the photo. My people will pick you up when I want you again."

Paul tried to think of something more to ask, but couldn't come up with anything.

"Paul, we'll be watching you. Your church? It's infested. Your home? It's infested. My people say you have a bug problem. Feel like you're being followed? You are."

CHAPTER 7

"All the leaves are brown..." Serena crooned into the microphone, aiming for a bluesy groove with her vocals.

"All the leaves are brown," her daughters echoed.

"And the sky is gray," she sang, feeling the lyrics heavily in her heart. Minnesota winters were harsh and long, so very long.

The girls echoed dispiritedly. Tom, their son, and their youngest daughter plucked away on their acoustic guitars. Serena tapped out a beat on the cowbell attachment on her snazzy red drum set, her Christmas present from Tom. Their eldest daughter played a pink electric guitar, which didn't really fit the sound of this particular song, but no one cared. With no audience to worry about, their standards were relaxed.

Last year, while acclimating to their new life in a rural area, and avoiding popular family activities where they would be seen by too many people, they joined a bluegrass group composed almost exclusively of friendly and warm senior citizens. The group welcomed their young son into the fold, teaching him how to play both the harmonica and the guitar. The rest of the family sat watching, week after week. Eventually the girls in the family felt comfortable singing along. Tom decided to take up an instrument, and was advised that the mandolin was an easy one to start with. After mandolin, he took up guitar.

One thing led to another, and before long the formerly-known-as Bridge family had evolved into their own family band. Now they stayed home and rehearsed their own line-up of songs. Sometimes they posted their sessions on the Internet to share with the world. By now, they didn't seriously fear that anyone would recognize them.

America, just one year after the bombing, had already changed so much that no one would care who they were, or what had happened back then when the world fell apart.

No, the Bridges would be left alone, and could probably shed their Meadows persona whenever they wanted. And they could leave Minnesota, where they were light and sun deprived and craving color.

But until Tom found a new job, here they were, suffering through another long frigid winter, with no warmth in sight. Jobs were hard to come by, and it would take a miracle to be on their way to a new life anytime soon. So, for now, they stayed in their roles as the Meadows family. To make themselves feel better they turned every light in the house on, lit their faux wood stove, and played music.

"I'd be safe and warm if I was in L.A."

"If I was in L.A.," the girls droned.

"California Dreamin' on such a winter's day…" Serena felt the tragedy of the song. There was no California post-bombing. Would life ever feel good again? How could the world recover from this evil? Would they ever recover?

She was shaken from her thoughts when the music came to an abrupt halt. She watched Tom bolt from the room. "Phone!" the kids yelled in unison.

Ah! Maybe a job offer! Serena prayed silently. Unbeknownst to her, their three kids were doing the same thing.

Tom was back in a flash. "Telemarketer."

Everyone groaned, wallowed in self-pity for a moment, and then started back up again, "All the leaves are brown…" Their session went on for four more songs before they wrapped up their evening.

They always ended with the song "I'll Fly Away", and since snacks followed their music session, everyone moved fast after hitting the final note, all leaving the room at the same time. By the time they hit the last verse, "Just a few more weary days and then, I'll fly away. To a land where joys shall never end. I'll fly away…" they were hungry.

They scrambled up the stairs and into the kitchen, but Serena had fallen short with the grocery shopping and hadn't prepared anything special for after-music snacks. Tom suggested that they go out, which was met with a round of cheers, a flurry of clothes-layering activity, and a mad dash to the mini-van, which was still drive-able, but barely. Once behind the wheel, he turned to Serena, "Where to? We could just go to Red Wing, or if you want to go someplace bigger we could go to the Cities."

The kids immediately voted for the Cities, and Serena had no objection. They set off down their long gravel driveway. The kids plugged in their iPods while Tom and Serena chatted. The forty-five mile road trip was comfortable, even though the skies weren't any cheerier than they'd been earlier in the day.

About half an hour into the trip, Tom interrupted Serena's passenger-side conversation with him mid-sentence. "I think we're being followed."

"What? What do you mean?"

"I know you haven't been Serena Wilcox, private detective, for over a decade, but haven't you noticed?" Tom glanced at the rearview mirror.

"No? You really think someone is following us?"

"Yeah. He was on our road. I figured he'd be turning off eventually, but he's still with us and we're already in Apple Valley."

"What are the odds someone would be on our road and still behind us? You must be right. Maybe someone saw us on those YouTube videos and recognized us. I knew we shouldn't have put those up there." Serena looked in the side-view mirror, wondering which car was tailing them.

"Why would anyone care about us?"

"I don't know. Following up on the arson? Which car is following us? The SUV right behind us?"

"No, he's three cars back now. I don't think it's about the arson. Could be someone we know?"

"Here in Minnesota? I don't think so. Everyone we've met here knows us as the Meadows. Besides, why would they follow us all the way to Apple Valley without signaling to us in some way?"

"What do you want me to do?"

The kids by now had taken interest in what their parents were talking about and all three were eavesdropping. Serena turned around in her seat to face them. "It'll be okay, don't worry." She looked at Tom and said, "Pull over in the next populated parking lot you see, pick a restaurant."

Tom came up on a restaurant quickly, as they were in the heart of Apple Valley. He parked the van in the first parking spot available. "What now?"

"Just wait. He'll come to the van."

A "gecko green" metallic VW beetle pulled into the parking lot and parked one space over.

"Is that him?"

"Yes."

"How could I have missed *that*?" Serena laughed.

"Because you're you."

The driver of the VW unfolded himself from the tiny car quickly and easily, with the agility of a teenager. He strode purposely over to the mini-van.

"But I never forget a face. I know that guy," Serena said quietly.

The young man approached the driver's side of the van and stood patiently waiting for Tom to open the window. Tom glanced at Serena.

"I'll explain later, go ahead and open the window," she said.

Tom pressed the button to let down the driver's side window, the only window control that was still operational on the mini-van. He looked expectantly at the blonde twenty-something man who was smiling at him.

"Hey, Tom, isn't it?" he began.

"I'm sorry, you are?"

"Otto. You probably noticed me following you back there."

"Yes. Your car stands out."

Otto grinned wider, looking like he'd been crowned Homecoming King. "Can we talk? Want to go in?" He nodded toward the Broadway Pizza entrance.

Tom looked at Serena, who nodded. "Sure," he said.

Otto didn't wait, but headed straight for the door. Tom closed the window and said, "How do you know him? Who is he?"

"Well, he's not Otto. He's Bryce. Or maybe he was lying the first time around. Or maybe he's not Bryce *or* Otto."

"You're sure you've seen this guy before?"

"Yes, sure. He was my server at the restaurant the night I was driving back from the fire. So maybe this *is* about the arson. Should we just go? Keep on driving and not come back?"

"No, let's hear what he has to say. He can find us again if we run."

"He doesn't look like somebody to be afraid of. We better go in, he'll wonder what's taking us so long."

The Bridge-Meadows family joined Bryce-Otto in the empty reception area of Broadway Pizza. After a few pleasantries were exchanged with the hostess, the group was seated. Serena initiated conversation as soon as the hostess left them alone.

"I recognize you, from about a year ago. You were at a Perkins, not too far from here. It was near Christmas. You were wearing a name tag that said Bryce, you were my server." Serena said this calmly, as smoothly as if she was talking about the weather.

Bryce-Otto looked surprised, but quickly recovered. "I didn't expect you to remember me. Yes, I was waiting tables there."

Tom said, "Why were you following us?"

"I was watching you before you torched your own house. Why did you do that, by the way?"

Tom and Serena didn't bother to disguise their horror. They didn't know what to say. What could they say?

Bryce-Otto laughed and clapped Tom on the shoulder. "Don't worry, man. I'm not after you or anything."

"What is this about?" Serena asked. She looked at her three kids- all three were noticeably frightened. None of them had spoken a word since they overheard that someone was following them.

"How did you know something was about to happen? We assume you faked your death because you thought someone would come after you? Why did you think that? What did you know, and how did you know it?" Otto-Bryce was suddenly serious now; his Homecoming King vibe had disappeared. In its place was an expression that transformed his features into a person who seemed both cunning and powerful.

"Who are you, really?" Serena asked.

"I work for someone important, let's leave it at that. Now, you obviously feel nervous right about now. You know- that I know- that you lit your house on fire and skipped out, created a new identity for yourselves and are hiding under Paul's mega-church, which is a fraud, by the way. He's a con man."

"We thought so," Tom said.

"They helped us hide. We haven't been to any of their meetings since that first month," Serena said defensively.

"We want you to go back."

"To the meetings?" asked Tom.

"Yes. We're watching Paul and his fugly brother Clyde. We need eyes and ears on him." Bryce-Otto halted his interrogation while their server took down their order. Serena ordered a deep dish Chicago style pizza, planning to eat very little of it. The last thing her stomach needed right now was pizza.

After the server had left, Bryce-Otto continued, "Let's go back to what you were doing when you torched your house. I was watching you then, you'd triggered off a few alarm bells in my organization."

"What organization is that?" asked Tom, knowing he was unlikely to get an honest answer.

"I'm not at liberty to say. But we were watching, looking for anyone showing signs of prior knowledge of the bombings. And you obviously knew something."

"And so did you. You couldn't do anything to stop it?" Serena countered.

"You didn't report anything. You lit your house on fire and ran." Bryce-Otto squinted up his eyes and fixed them into a stare that was intended to intimidate Serena, but failed to do so.

"What could I say that anyone would believe? I was watching the news; I had a really bad feeling. I had a vivid nightmare that I felt was prophetic, but I'm no psychic, at least not proven to be. I had a couple dreams that relatives died, and then they did, but, they were sick at the time so it was kind of a logical conclusion. I dreamed that the United States was going to be hit with nuclear bombs, and I believed the dream was real. We took a leap of faith that my dream was a real warning, and we did what we could to keep our family safe."

"And your husband went along with this? You burned down your own house based on a dream? And safe from what? You were already in a safe area of the country. Why move? Why hide?" Bryce-Otto shook his head. "I don't believe you. You knew something. What did you know, and how did you know it?"

"Safe from the government," said Tom.

"I had a bad feeling that the government was going to fall apart after the nuclear bombings, and that we'd be better off if we were not in the system. I can't explain why, just a bad feeling," Serena insisted.

Bryce-Otto looked from Tom to Serena; and back again. "I can't tell if you people are crazy and delusional, or if you're lying. If you're crazy, you got it right – bombs happened. WWIII, everything hit the fan. So you're not crazy. Which means you must be lying, because I don't believe in that psychic dream crap you're giving me."

"My mom isn't lying. She had a dream. And we left because something bad was going to happen," Carrie spoke up, causing everyone at the table to look at her. She stared back at all the faces. "Well, it's true. My parents are not crazy, and they are not lying."

Bryce-Otto leaned across the table and said in a raspy whisper, "Tell me about your mother's friend. The one she e-mails in Iran. Her friend have a dream too?"

Serena froze for half a second, and then she began to sing, "Just a few more weary days and then, I'll fly away…"

Her singing caught Bryce-Otto off guard and he sat stunned, as the girls' voices joined in.

"To a land where joys shall never end, I'll fly away…"

And on that note, the family did what they always did after singing that song. They left the room with great haste. The surprise factor gave them only a few seconds lead, but it was enough time to get into the van and lock the doors before Bryce-Otto reached them. He put his face two inches from Tom's window and yelled, "I know where you live!"

"Just go, go!" urged Serena.

Tom drove, and drove. They looked over their shoulders every few minutes. No VW beetle, of any color. "Where do we go? Our safe house is not safe anymore."

"Let's take Karyn up on her offer to visit."

"You have her address?"

"She lives up North, a cabin in Deer River, near Bowstring Lake."

"We won't get there until after midnight. Will she be okay with that?"

"She'll have to be."

CHAPTER 8

After driving for about five hours, the Bridge-Meadows family arrived at the lakeside cabin where Karyn lived with her husband Dan and four children. "Cabin" was a misleading description. Their home was impressive – large and rambling with many levels. There was a family room, living room, sitting area, large open kitchen, and enough space to sleep about a dozen people. Serena thought the cabin looked like a bed and breakfast hotel, generously roomy for a single family home.

"Wow, this is really nice," said Carrie. She squinted at the fully lit front entrance. Even the landscaping was illuminated, with soft solar lighting along the pathway to the door.

Serena glanced at her three children, who all looked a little rough around the edges after their harrowing exit from the restaurant the day before, traveling into the wee hours of the night, and sleeping on and off with their heads mashed against whatever they could find to lean on. Well, this wasn't a reunion, and besides, Karyn was not a pretentious person, or at least not the Karyn she remembered.

Serena reached out to ring the doorbell, but before she could press the button, Karyn flung the door open wide. "Serena! You made it!" She ushered the family in.

"Is that coffee I smell?" asked Tom.

"Karyn, you do realize we've imposed upon you at 2:30 in the morning?" Serena laughed. She couldn't believe the feast she saw for them on the table. Artfully arranged on a country checked tablecloth was a bowl of fruit containing perfectly ripened bananas, deep purple grapes, and red apples worthy of Snow White's temptation, a basket of assorted breads with a side dish of butter pats and jellies, a tier of three different varieties of breakfast muffins, a pitcher of what appeared to be fresh-squeezed orange juice in a bucket of ice, serving dishes, cloth napkins, and elegant long stemmed glassware – all waiting for Serena and her family to consume it.

"I'll take you any time, day or night. It's been too long, dear friend!" Karyn threw her arms around Serena for a quick power hug, a tight squeeze that projected puppy-like affection. "Sit, sit," she said to the rag-tag group. "Dig in, whatever you want. Tom, you wanted coffee? I did make some. How about you, Serena?"

"Yes, I'll take a coffee, thanks," she said. Tom and Serena chose to remain standing, after having been cramped in the car for too many hours. The three kids sat and shyly helped themselves to the buffet. The adults stood quietly for several minutes, content to bask in the relief of having reached their destination.

"Hey, you made it!" Dan's booming voice preceded his appearance in the kitchen. "So, what's going on? Why are you here at two-something in the middle of the night?"

"Dan!" Karyn admonished him as she returned from getting the coffee, but she waited expectantly for an answer.

"Well, it's about you, actually," said Serena, as she received a mug of hot coffee from Karyn.

"About me? But it's been forever since I was your partner, and your cases weren't anything that would come back to haunt me."

"No, it's not about our private detective work."

"Then what is it about?" asked Dan, without waiting for an answer. "I made a fire in the living room. We can talk in there." He looked at the three kids sitting at his table, as if it was the first he noticed their presence. "Kids, there's a TV if you want to find something to watch. We have a game system too. Whatever you want."

"Dan, it's the middle of the night. I made up beds for them. They probably want to sleep," said Karyn.

"Thank you. They'll be fine, we can talk in the other room," said Serena. "But we can't stay long, they'll be looking for us."

"What?" Dan was startled. "Who's looking for you?"

The four adults left the kids to their buffet and sank their bodies into the pair of matching overstuffed suede sofas facing the fire. "We don't know for sure that they'll come here," said Tom.

"Yes we do. They know who you are," said Serena. She stirred her coffee to mix the sugar and cream, and took a few sips.

"Start at the beginning, how is this about me?" asked Karyn.

"It's about your adventure in Kish," Serena said.

"Oh no, why?" said Karyn. She avoided looking at Dan.

"Kish, the gorgeous island in Iran, where the snorkeling is the best in the world? And you went there because Kish doesn't require a visa, right?" asked Serena.

"We didn't have time for visas, it was a spur of the moment thing," said Karyn. "If I'd known how dangerous it was to go there, I wouldn't have done it."

"And if I'd known that Karyn wasn't going to be allowed at the beach, I wouldn't have gone snorkeling. I had no idea she was going to be shuttled off to the 'women's beach'. I shouldn't have gone off without her, especially after they gave her a scarf to cover her head. I should have known better than to leave her there." said Dan.

"I was the one who wanted to linger in the shops. It wasn't your fault," said Karyn. "The women's beach was lovely. There was nothing about it that sounded off any alarm bells."

"I'm not blaming either of you for what happened," said Serena. "I'm just giving a recap: Karyn ended up taken to Tehran, to a safe house. How she got there is not your fault. Kish is a hotbed of smuggling and terrorist activity. You didn't expect her to be taken, but she was."

"Nothing was ever done about it. They released her, brought her back to Kish, dropped her off at the hotel we were registered with, and we never knew why they took her, or who they were. Our government made some empty promises to look into it, and that was it," said Dan.

"But I was safe, and that's all that really matters. Why is this coming up?" asked Karyn, still avoiding looking directly at her husband.

"Yes, I know, not your fault. But, you might remember that when Karyn got back to the island, she went to the Kish Cyber Café at Shayan Hotel, where she sent me several e-mails," Serena continued. "These e-mails were apparently read by more people than just me."

"They probably read everything in that Café," said Tom.

"Who's 'they'?" asked Dan.

"I don't know. Our government is involved, either directly or indirectly," said Serena.

"Which one? The Williams camp or the Kinji camp?" asked Dan.

"My guess would be the Williams camp, but I don't know," said Serena.

"I don't understand any of this. The only person I e-mailed was you. I don't remember my exact words, do you?" asked Karyn. "Why are they interested in this now? That was over ten years ago."

"They think I knew something about Iran before the bombings," said Serena. She locked into Karyn's eyes and held steady eye contact for a few long seconds until Karyn squirmed and looked away.

"Oh." Karyn's voice was barely above a whisper.

"Honey? What is this about?" asked Dan. "Karyn? Is there something you want to tell me?"

"Should we leave the room while you two talk about this?" asked Serena, hoping to escape the awkwardness that was sure to follow.

"No, no, you can stay," said Karyn. "Dan, I didn't want to say anything because you felt bad enough about me being abducted."

"What happened?" asked Dan.

"The head scarf they gave me at the island was slipping and getting in my face, so while I was at the safe house I took it off," said Karyn. "That made the guards mad. One of them yanked my head back by grabbing the hair on the back of my head, and the other one spit in my face. That's all that –"

"He spit in your face! When were you going to tell me this?" Dan yelled. He was up now, pacing the room.

"Uh, never. I didn't think you ever needed to know," said Karyn.

"Tell me the rest of it," said Dan in a normal tone of voice, sitting back down.

"The guards must have been feeling cocky because they started running off at the mouth. One of them said, 'Americans will not be so bold when so many die.' And the other said, 'We bomb them their Holy Day and they will cover heads.' And then they laughed," said Karyn. "It was all in English, so they wanted me to hear them."

"And you wrote this in an e-mail?" asked Dan. "And this was nothing important? Don't you think 'bomb' and 'Americans die" could be the keywords that triggered you as a terrorist? Come on, Karyn!" Dan jumped off the couch again to pace the floor space between the sofas and the fireplace, which had dwindled down to ashes but no one noticed or cared.

"Wait, wait! I don't think Karyn is on a terrorist watch list. They'd have come to her before now if she was," said Serena.

"Then what's going on? What else don't I know?" Dan asked.

"I'm going to go check on the kids," mumbled Tom. He made a hasty retreat out of the uncomfortable room.

Serena looked at the two of them. "I'll go see if Tom needs any help with the kids." She hadn't made it out of the room yet before she heard Dan bellow, "You did WHAT?"

Shortly afterward, the house was awake. Dan and Karyn's children seemed to pour in from all corners of the house, scrambling toward their parents. Tom and Serena stayed out of the fray, tucking their own kids in for the night and quickly joining them. They lay in the guest bed, trying to shut out the noise from the other room, but it was impossible. First there was a flurry of parental duty as Dan and Karyn divided the children and escorted them back to their rooms, next came the conversation that Serena and Tom were hoping to miss.

"Okay, back up. So you are saying that not only did you hear that the Iranians were going to bomb us, but you've been talking to them for all these years?" asked Dan, forgetting to keep his voice down.

"I've not been talking to *them*! I said I met a nice lady there. I gave her my e-mail address. She started writing to me," said Karyn.

"While you were in the safe house, being tortured, you made a friend."

"I was not tortured. The hair pulling and spitting was the only thing that ever happened. I would have told you if anything really bad happened."

"Really? You would have?" scoffed Dan.

"Look, I know you're mad. I should have told you, but you already felt so responsible that I was taken in the first place. I thought it would make things worse if you knew about the spitting."

"And the bombing, you couldn't mention that?"

"Not without telling you about the spitting."

"And your Iranian mole friend? You couldn't work that in either?"

"Not without the spitting. I'm sorry, Dan. I should have told you. And she's not a mole. She's an ordinary citizen."

"Everything makes sense now. That's how Serena knew that something bad was going to happen, why she burned her house down and went into hiding. I knew she wasn't psychic! I've been such an idiot."

"I forwarded the e-mails Farideh sent me to Serena. And you're right, that's why she went into hiding. She encouraged me to do the same, which is why I wanted to stay here, and pull back from society. I figured we were pretty safe in such a remote location by the lake."

"And you never filled me in, all because you lied about being manhandled in Iran? Or as you call it, the spitting."

"Yes. One lie led to another, and then I didn't know how to tell you. I knew you'd be mad."

"You're right. I'm mad."

The two sat in silence for so long that Tom fell asleep. Serena stayed alert, even though she was resting. Time was of the essence. She was giving the couple a few more moments alone only because she felt guilty for her part in keeping secrets. She had advised Karyn to tell Dan at the very start, but when Karyn was too insecure to do it, Serena had played along. She regretted that, but it was all in the past now.

Just when she thought she would need to help things along, the couple resumed talking. "How long will you stay mad at me?" Karyn asked, her voice choked up with tears.

"Come here," Dan pulled Karyn closer to him. "I can't stay mad at you, you know that. That's why you should have told me. What did your friend say that convinced you that the Iranians were going to do this?"

"Farideh said that everyone was talking about it. There was a date – the right one, by the way. Everyone knew, and there was no doubt it was true, that these bombings were going to happen. They were saying 'Death to America' in the streets," said Karyn.

"But they've always said things like that, how did you know it was the real deal?"

"I'll show you the e-mail that Farideh sent me, the one that I forwarded to Serena. It is long, and it is convincing."

"You saved it? And you didn't send it to the FBI or at least the police?"

"Dan, I did send it to the FBI! I got a confirmation e-mail back. They said they sent the information to Homeland Security."

"You have that e-mail saved too?" asked Serena. Her presence startled both of them and they jumped.

"Yes, I still have the e-mail. I save everything."

"That's exactly what they're afraid of – they wonder what you have. They'll be here soon. Back up your computer files, now."

"Who's they?" asked Dan for the second time.

"I don't know. Really, Dan, there are no more secrets. You are all caught up to where we are. Well, you will be after you read Farideh's e-mail. But no time for that now. Grab a flash drive and get your files. I have my own flash drive in my purse. I need a copy of the files too. Then – wipe your computer clean."

"I don't know how to do that," said Karyn.

"Don't look at me," said Dan.

"For that, I'll wake up my son. He can do it. The main thing is that we get those files. Now."

CHAPTER 9

>>My Karyn,

I write you heavy heart. You must know for it is my hope you can go safe.

Iran make fools of everyone. For years they lie about nuclear missiles. Nuclear Nonproliferation Treaty is nothing, they spit upon it as easily as they spit on you, dear Karyn.

They threaten who wants make peace with Israel. Pro-West Arab Saudi Arabia and Egypt see Iran success nuclear, but have no fight. Iran pressure Lebanon, Syria, the Palestinians, and the Iraqis. Many thousands, hundred thousands, join radical Islamist. "Death to America!" on Iranian street for too many year. No one stop Iran. Now they make nuclear weapons in short period. They make stockpiles uranium for nuclear device in few months—make nuclear weapons in short period. They make centrifuges to pipe work. They learn technology when they talk to UN, many lies. Now they can do bomb. They will do this. It will be soon. I hear it from husband. You trust me to know truth. I tell you day and time. I tell you where missiles strike. You go safe.

Your Farideh <<

Paul read the forwarded e-mail over and over again, but still didn't understand why someone had sent it to him. His head was swimming with theories that fell apart. What had begun as a simple blackmail plot to get himself onto Kinji's staff had evolved into playing serious dirty politics with the big boys.

When Paul had scoffed at President William's speech that day on the tarmac, he had no idea that he was being watched, and followed, the entire time. Of *course* William's people tracked every onlooker, how could he have thought otherwise? It had been foolish for Paul to show up there, expecting to go unnoticed. It was probably that very move that got him discovered, although the jig would have been up anyway, since William's team had Kinji's office bugged.

The wind out of his sails, he didn't trust himself to pinpoint the exact moment of his downfall. He sat with slumped shoulders, waiting to be told what to do next, like the minion he was destined to be.

The phone rang. He answered with trepidation, having a strong feeling that the sender of the e-mail would be on the other end of the line. He was not mistaken.

"You opened the e-mail."

"Yes? What is that?"

"It's a big problem for the President."

"For Williams?"

"Yes, for Williams."

"What does this have to do with me?"

"You're going to be the one to fix it."

"How do I do that?"

"Go outside. I'm standing in your yard, in the back of your house."

Paul was only a few feet away from his back door. He peered out the window and didn't see anyone. He slowly opened the door and saw a young blonde man sitting on one of Paul's own lawn chairs that he'd placed amongst the landscaped shrubbery, well concealed from the road. He studied the man's face until recognition washed over him. "I know you. You're the intern I saw that day on the tarmac. You got the podium ready for William's speech."

"I'm more than an intern," Bryce scoffed.

"Obviously. So what's your deal?" Paul picked up a second chair, walked to where Bryce was, sat upon it, and leaned in close, conspiringly, "We're both players. We even look alike enough to pass for brothers. So why are you sitting in the power seat when I'm sitting in a puddle of drool?"

"Why should I tell you anything? You work for me."

Paul shrugged to feign indifference, not even fooling himself. "I was just curious."

"How did I succeed where you have failed? What have I got that you don't?" Bryce smiled with the same full wattage he'd flashed months ago in the restaurant, when showing Serena his frat-boy good teeth, but this time his smile was sinister; a gleam shone on his canines, accentuating his wolf-like grin.

"Ouch, I wouldn't have put that fine of a point on it," said Paul.

Bryce backed his chair away from Paul's invasion of his personal space and said, "I'm here, and you're there," pointing his right index finger like a gloved Dr. Seuss character, first at Paul and then back to himself, "because I am John's nephew. You are nothing more than a pretender."

The light dawned. Blue blood, nothing Paul could do about that. He could curse his lot in life, but where would it get him? Scratching and clawing and conning his way up had at least gotten him this far, sitting with President John William's right hand man, his own kin no less. It wasn't over for Paul yet.

So the Kinji plan failed, who cares? He'd gotten away with it, no harm done. And now he was in William's camp. Did it matter to him which President he was barnacling himself to? Tuh-may-toe, tuh-mah-toe. He reassessed his situation in milliseconds and said, with a condescending tone, "I see things clearly now."

Bryce reddened and his jaw clenched with unmistakable anger. "He doesn't partner with me because I'm family. I'm good for it."

Paul smiled, patronizing him now. My, how this felt good. Bryce was easily played. For all of his bravado, Bryce was nothing more than a punk kid with ego issues. This would be easier than he thought to extract information. "Oh really? You don't really know anything, do you? You told me that's all I need to know because you don't know it yourself." Paul folded his arms across his chest, sat there grinning like the Cheshire Cat, and waited for Bryce to take the bait.

Bryce leaned forward, his eyes narrowed into angry slits. "The e-mail was sent before the Big War, and was forwarded to FBI. We knew, we knew about the attacks before they happened."

Paul struggled to maintain a strong poker face. He was blown away by this, it was much bigger than what he expected to hear; although he had no clue what to expect, he didn't expect this. Wow. Mind blowing. So we knew. Why didn't we stop it? We *couldn't* stop it? Or we *wouldn't* stop it? Aloud he said, "You've got me. That's big stuff. Okay, you're a bona fide insider, not just the nephew."

Bryce relaxed his posture and smiled easily, baring no teeth. "No more questions. Now I tell you what to do, and you do it."

"Got it. What do you want me to do? Find out who sent this e-mail? Or who it was sent to?"

"No, we already know both. The sender is an Iranian woman, the receiver is her American friend. The American friend has another friend we've been watching. She could be a problem."

"You want me to follow her? Keep an eye on her?"

Bryce grinned with his lips curled back, his wolf smile back in full wattage. "No, we want you to kill her."

"What? Seriously? I'm not a hit man." Paul was too stunned to think of a way out of this slippery hole he was falling into, but he knew he couldn't kill someone, especially a woman!

"We need her taken out."

"Come on, she's talked to people. I can't kill everyone who knows about the e-mail," Paul protested.

"Don't worry about that. I will threaten everyone she's told. When she's dead, they'll know I mean business."

"How do you know who she's told? And why not kill her yourself?"

"I've been following her for a while, and have her place bugged. She keeps to herself. She's told her husband, that's it. Other than him, there's the friend who forwarded the email, and her husband. Three people left after she's gone. And if they act squirrely, we'll kill them too before they can talk to anyone else."

"Why trust them at all? Kill them now. Or is the body count of innocent people getting too high?"

"Get off your high horse -- you're scum. If you weren't, we wouldn't have tapped you for this."

"And if I don't do it?"

"I'll find someone else who will. You'll go to prison for the Kinji blackmail. And while in prison…"

"I'll have an accident?"

"You catch on fast. So we have a deal?"

"What choice do I have?" asked Paul weakly. Again he was bested… and this time he couldn't con his way back into the power seat.

CHAPTER 10

"Clyde, I'm in trouble," Paul began. The brothers were in their parents' kitchen again. Clyde was frying bacon and making coffee while Paul leaned heavily on the table, standing over it with both arms locked at the elbows, hands planted on the tablecloth with fingers outstretched. His head was hanging low, his boyish locks falling forward. Clyde thought he looked about twelve. Bailing him out of trouble had been as routine then as it was now. "Did you hear me, Clyde?"

"I heard you. I knew you were in trouble the moment you walked in the door. I told you not to do that Kinji thing. She's smart and a woman, two reasons why she's not worth it."

"No, it's not her. John Williams is blackmailing me. He found out what I was doing."

"What? How did he know?" Paul had Clyde's full attention now.

"He has a bug in Kinji's office. He knew everything, and he had me in his cross hairs."

"What does he want with you?" Clyde felt a familiar stirring within him. It was the same force that had led him to despicable acts in the past; all to protect his little brother… or, maybe, it was beyond that. It was a hunger, a craving, and his protective nature was an excuse? Possibly, but why then did he not act on these urges unless Paul was in trouble? No, this was about protecting family. Clyde was not a psycho, of that he was sure.

"He wants me to kill somebody."

"He what?" Clyde laughed, thinking Paul was making a clever joke. He had him going, what a corker that brother of his. Clyde laughed until his belly shook. Only when he stopped to take a breath did he notice that Paul wasn't laughing with him. Paul was still frozen in his stance over the table, arms holding his body up, head bent; a beaten man, a scared man, a fugitive. Clyde sank into a kitchen chair, the bacon left to grow cold on the counter.

"He sent his nephew to give me the message. If I don't kill Serena Wilcox, he'll have me put in prison and then they'll have me killed in there, in prison."

"Serena who?"

"She's a former private detective. She's one of ours, Clyde."

"What do you mean, one of ours? Our Off Grid people?"

"Yes. She has three kids, husband. We set them up in Goodhue. We gave them the new name of Meadows. Before that they were the Browns, no, the Bridges."

"Okay, yeah, I think I know who you're talking about. Why do they want her dead? What does she know?"

"She knows something big, Clyde. I can't believe it. The government knew about the attacks before they happened. She has proof, e-mail proof sent from an Iranian woman."

"Our government?"

"Yes, our own. We knew and didn't do anything."

Clyde sucked air between his teeth and then exhaled slowly with a prolonged wispy whistle. "Paul, they were never after you. They were following *her*. We made it easy for them. They've been watching us all along. They know me too, don't they?"

"Yes, they know you. They know about your computer lab, and they're calling Off Grid a cult."

"It is a cult. Sort of, anyway. Just a big sham, and I suppose they know that too, don't they?"

"They know all about us, they think we're buffoons. When I showed up at the tarmac, they had to be laughing their asses off."

"We know nothing about them. That will change."

Paul finally freed himself from his vigil at the table and sat in the chair across from his brother. He stared at his empty plate, and as if Clyde could read his thoughts, bacon suddenly appeared on it. He ate three strips, one after the other, and then spoke, "Clyde, this is bigger than my problems in the past. We're talking about killing a person."

Clyde raised his eyebrows and snorted. "And what makes you think I haven't done that for you before?"

Paul stared at Clyde. He knew it was no joke. The repressed memory of what John Williams said to him came back. *My people tell me that your only childhood connection to Kinji is a babysitter in common. A Mrs. Mason, who we'd have talked to, but she's deceased. Died from a freak accident in the home.*

Clyde cleared the plates and loaded the dishwasher. He let the information settle, knowing that Paul would accept the situation and would move on if given enough time to digest it, process it. He was Clyde, the big protective brother. He only did what needed to be done. If Paul didn't see that now, he would come around to it eventually, of that Clyde was certain.

"Mrs. Mason?" Paul croaked. He tried to don his poker face, but he couldn't con a con, especially the better of the two of them.

"Don't look so shocked, Paul. The old bat had it coming. She did it to herself. No one messes with my brother."

"Is she the only one?" *Please, please let her be the only one,* thought Paul.

Clyde smiled gently, placating a child. "If that's what you need to hear, we'll leave it at that. Let's move on. We have a serious situation on our hands."

Paul's self-preservation instincts kicked in and this time he was successful at putting on his best poker face. Never show your true feelings to a sociopath, especially if he is also your brother. As Paul's life was crashing down on him, he still felt that Clyde was his best, and only, option. "What do we do?"

"Well, we don't kill her."

"We don't?" Paul was careful not to let relief creep into his voice.

"No, we let *him* do it."

"Him?"

"John Williams. We'll bring the girl to the President himself."

"What? Why would we do this? Wouldn't he have us all killed? And how would we even get close enough to him? I only got close because he nabbed me. And before that, they must have let me get close, because they knew who I was, and they were following me. They won't let me near them if they don't want me there."

"We go through his nephew. We get the nephew, then he'll want to see us. He gets the nephew and the girl. Lets us go. That's the deal. We won't kill her, that's what they want us to do."

"Yes, I know that's what they want. I don't get what you are saying. Even if we manage to get both of them, and get them to the President, and go as far as making the deal, wouldn't they kill us after they got what they wanted?"

"Paul, they want to frame you for the murder. They get rid of both of you that way. They'll kill you, you know. But if you refuse to kill her, and they have to go another way, you have leverage."

"They'll just kill me anyway, remember? If not on the spot, they'll get me for the blackmail attempt and kill me in prison."

"No, they won't. You will have too much information on them, with the proof uploaded to our computer lab. Our kid hackers are very good, Paul. They can get them at their own game. They'll have everything recorded in the cloud, so to speak, including the e-mail they sent you – you still have it right? Why did they get sloppy about that, did they think we wouldn't forward it, save it, copy it?"

"I don't know, maybe they made a mistake. The nephew is cocky. He might be going off the rule book."

"They won't be able to get their fingers on all the recordings, they'll be digitally floating everywhere and anywhere, all timed to be released should something happen to you."

"Recordings? All I have is the e-mail."

"I'm talking about what we will have, what the kids will get for us. They'll love this project. I'll tell them they'll get college credit for it."

"So they get the girl, we get left alone. Why should we give them the girl at all? I don't like getting a woman killed, a mother with three kids."

"It's the fastest way out of this. They want you because of her. Sever that connection."

"Then we leave the country?"

"They can find us anywhere, even in the remotest of African villages. But it's unnecessary to hide. What will keep us safe is our insurance policy. We blackmail them, we stay safe."

"Blackmail didn't work out so well for me, remember?"

"That's because you didn't have me running the show. Don't worry, little brother, I've got your back. This will work. I'll talk to my pimply faced hackers and get them on it. They'll have you all suited up to record everything."

"What if they check for bugs?"

Clyde winked. "You haven't met Nicholas, my best – he's the new kid. That boy is a magician. He'll put a bug in play that not even you will know is there."

"They'll scan."

"Not an issue. He has a remote controlled bug; that looks like an actual bug. He can fly it remotely, very remotely. He programs the thing and it can transmit from wherever it is, from long range too. We can bring it with us; release it before meeting their people. It's so small it's nearly invisible to the naked eye, and it's fast."

"I don't know, it's the President's security detail, they probably have ways."

"The bug is fast, it'll zip right by them. You'll see, it will work." Clyde rubbed his hands together gleefully. At heart, he was a computer nerd too, but he was born too late to take to computers as naturally as the younger generation. He lived vicariously through his dream team of young geniuses.

Paul shook his head in amazement. "Where did you get these kids anyway? How do you get them to do what you want? They aren't on payroll."

"Funny how building a state of the art lab can reel them in. Free lab time is enough, and I do pay them a little something out of my pocket. If I bring in pizza, they're happy to stay all night long."

"I never knew how you got them there. I never knew a lot of things," said Paul.

"You aren't still hung up on old Mrs. Mason, are you? I only do what's necessary. You trust me, don't you Paulie?"

"Yes, I trust you Clyde."

"Then we'll get the kids to set us up with everything we need, and find the nephew and the girl for us. I'll get the nephew. You get Serena-whatsherface. I'm sure you can talk her into coming to our place. She knows you."

CHAPTER 11

Serena belted herself into the passenger's seat. "Where are we going?"

"I was hoping you'd tell me," said Tom.

"We can't go home if Bryce, or Otto – let's call him Bryce – knows where we live."

"He seems able to find us anywhere. Let's go home. We can secure the house."

"What do you mean by 'secure the house'?"

"What do you think I use to shoot at coyotes and raccoons?"

"You wouldn't really shoot Bryce, would you?"

"Sure I would, if it's him or you."

"You're going to walk around all the time holding a gun?"

"I can booby-trap the house."

"How?"

"I can do it."

"Home does sound good. Our own bed, our coffee, our food."

"I want to go home," chimed in all three kids from the back. Ipod and tablet earbuds were temporarily removed. Unplugging happened when their parents said something they wanted to hear.

Home was agreed upon and they drove the six hours back from Deer River, making a stop at the McDonald's in Cannon Falls. After a trip to the restrooms, the Meadows family wandered back to the parking lot, carrying drinks and bags of food. They stopped short when approached by a familiar figure.

"Hey, Meadows-es!" Paul rang out cheerfully. "Long time no see. Haven't seen you around seminar lately." He didn't wait for a reply, but clapped his hand on Tom's shoulder. "How's the place in Goodhue working out?"

"It was great, until people found us," said Tom.

Paul didn't need to feign surprise, because he *was* surprised to hear that they were already aware of discovery. *Who was after them? Was Paul their second choice? Or had Bryce laid down the foundation for Paul to close the deal on?* It was infuriating to be out of the loop. However, he bounced back quickly, and feeling a grin not unlike the Grinch's spreading over his face, he came up with a plan. It was too, too easy. "Wow, we can't have you in a dangerous situation. Follow me back to my place. We can talk there and figure out a plan to relocate you." Whatever possessed him to strike up a spontaneous conversation in a "chance meeting" location had produced brilliant results. This was most unexpected, especially since he hadn't really thought this through ahead of time. He hadn't worked up how to get Serena. He'd simply gotten lucky.

"Oh, that would be perfect," said Serena. "Thank you."

As Paul headed back to his own vehicle he reflected on his good fortune and dug into his pocket for his phone. He had only one number programmed, Clyde's. He dialed it now. Clyde picked up after the first bar of the "Everybody Wants to Rule the World" ringtone he'd assigned to Paul's number.

"You rang?"

"I got them. The Meadows family will be at our place in about fifteen minutes."

"The whole clan, not just the girl?"

"Serena."

"Doesn't matter, I'll deal with the collateral damage."

"Collateral damage? What?"

"Put them in the kitchen, give them some coffee, milk for the kids. There's a bag of chips in the pantry. Keep them happy and talking. Stall. I'm thirty miles out."

"Did you get your job done?"

"Where do you think I've been?"

"So you've got Bryce with you?"

"He's in the trunk."

"In the trunk!"

"He's not dead, you moron! I shoved him in there to put the fear of God in him."

"I don't think you know anything about God."

"And you do?"

"You threw me with the trunk thing. Sorry."

"He's cramped in there, not much air to breathe. He'll be humble by the time I get him home. Humble and ready to chat."

"I should have known that you knew what you were doing, sorry I doubted you," Paul said, his voice dripping with contrition. *Hold on, Paul, don't let him know you're unnerved*, he scolded himself.

"Apology accepted. See you in a few minutes. Show time!" Clyde tossed his phone onto the empty passenger's seat beside him, forgetting to disconnect the call.

Paul began to disconnect from his end, but hesitated when he heard noise. *He forgot to end the call.* Paul could hear clicking sounds and then dialogue:

An unknown female voice: "Why didn't you write me? Why? It wasn't over for me, I waited for you for seven years. But now it's too late."

An unknown male voice, with Clyde's voice saying the same words along with him: "I wrote you 365 letters. I wrote you every day for a year."

The same female voice again: "You wrote me?"

Male, again with Clyde: "Yes... it wasn't over, it still isn't over."

What IS this? I recognize this. Paul scratched his brain trying to come up with it. *I've got it! This is from "The Notebook". My deranged brother is playing audio tracks from "The Notebook" and is quoting it from memory as it plays.* Paul disconnected the call before he could hear any more.

The Meadows following behind Paul noticed that he was on the phone. "I wonder who he's talking to, maybe he's setting something new up for us already," said Serena.

"Maybe. Good thing we ran into him, huh?"

"That was strange though, don't you think? We've never run into him randomly before. What are the odds of a chance meeting, really?"

"Providence?"

"Or?"

"Not? You think he was following us? Why would he do that? Are you sure you aren't paranoid?"

"I don't know, seems like a big coincidence to me. We know for sure that Bryce was following us, and then Paul just happens to show up where we are. What if they are working together?"

"It would explain why our safe house isn't safe."

"I think we should assume we can't trust anybody at this point."

"Better safe than sorry?"

"So what do we do?"

Tom slowed down, letting a car slip between him and Paul. "I don't know."

"There's not much traffic on these roads, it's not like you can get lost in the crowd. You won't even have another traffic light between here and there."

"I have a gun with me."

"You *what*?"

"I was in the Army, I'm not Barney Fife."

"So it's loaded then?"

"That's how it works."

"What if the kids had gotten it out?"

"Our kids wouldn't touch a gun."

"We wouldn't," came from the backseat.

"Don't ever, ever touch a gun," said Serena, turning around in her seat to address the kids. "Maybe we should have them stay in the car."

"Good idea. You guys stay in the car."

"One problem, how are you going to bring that in there? It's a hunting rifle, not like you can hide it."

"Not the rifle. I bought a handgun." He lifted up his shirt to expose the handle.

Serena's jaw dropped and she gasped in a dramatic how-dare-you exclamation. "A handgun!"

"We're here. Kids, stay in the car. Serena, stay in the car." Tom stopped the vehicle and quickly stepped out.

"No, I'm going in too. Kids, stay in the car. Don't open the door for anybody but us." Serena got out of the car and followed her husband onto the front walk where Paul was standing, waiting.

"The kids are welcome to come in, too," said Paul, smiling like a good host.

"They're doing their own thing, they'll be fine while we talk," Serena said, while walking toward the front door.

Both she and Tom looked expectantly at Paul to open the door.

Paul looked back at their vehicle and could see the kids' heads bent over books and handheld gadgets. Satisfied that there was no reason to bring the kids into this, and hoping that Clyde would see it the same way, he let Serena and Tom into the house. He ushered the pair into the kitchen and offered them coffee.

"No thank you," said Serena. Even though coffee did sound good, she didn't want anything from this man.

"I'll take a cup," said Tom.

Serena glared at him. Tom met that glare and raised one eyebrow that said, "Why not?"

Paul studied the coffee maker, not sure how to proceed. Clyde always made the coffee. This wasn't rocket science, he told himself. He found the filter basket, put a fresh filter in, and took a guess on how much coffee to put in. He filled the back with water and turned the switch. *That was easy, why did I wait for Clyde all those times I wanted coffee?*

As the coffee machine gargled and spit its brew Paul gathered up the sugar bowl and two mugs. He set them on the table, glancing briefly at his captives. He considered himself to be pretty good at reading people, and these two were completely clueless. He would have no problem keeping them here until Clyde returned.

Serena studied Paul as he bustled about the kitchen. She considered herself to be pretty good at reading people, and she could tell that he was definitely involved. What his involvement was, she didn't know, but he was not to be trusted. She made eye contact with Tom, using their been-married-for-a-long-time silent language to say, "You might need that gun." Then she made the most of Paul having his back turned to them by examining everything around her.

She noticed a roster of Off Grid Ghost members. If Paul left the room she planned to snoop through it. Maybe Bryce, or Otto, was in the roster. Of course, someone going by two different names could easily invent a third name. The roster was probably useless. She looked around the room for another clue. Something, anything, to give her an idea of what Paul was up to.

She wondered whose taste was reflected in the kitchen. A collection of country roosters including a rooster salt and pepper shaker, a rooster cookie jar, and a rooster planter? Really? Whose kitchen was this? Did Paul have a significant other? She didn't think so. Her eyes rested on the framed photos on the wall. Ah-ha! Pictures of three little boys, all in plaid suits too large for them.

Family picture taken later, with two of the boys, now older, one whose face was clearly Paul's. So this was his parents' house. Finding nothing else of interest in the kitchen, Serena asked where the bathroom was.

Paul, suspecting her motives not at all, directed her down the hall and to the right. Serena went promptly down the hall and to the left, where the door to the office was open. A netbook was on a small table with the lid open. Serena looked over her shoulder – she couldn't see the kitchen from where she was. She ventured in. What she saw on the screen caused her to temporarily stop breathing:

>>My Karyn,

I write you heavy heart. You must know for it is my hope you can go safe.

Iran make fools of everyone. For years they lie about nuclear missiles. Nuclear Nonproliferation Treaty is nothing, they spit upon it as easily as they spit on you, dear Karyn ... >>

CHAPTER 12

President Ann Kinji didn't feel presidential at the moment. She hadn't felt presidential since she'd seen the picture of her best friend and husband with a little girl who was most certainly his daughter. She had been wrestling with indecision about how to respond for three sleepless days and nights. Between the anxiety and the sleep deprivation, her briefings with staff, ambassadors, governors, military heads, and the UN were impossible: her mind was drifting away, consumed with thoughts of a child she didn't know about, a child she wished was her own, but nonetheless was living proof that her marriage was over, and apparently had been for years.

She had to nip this thing in the bud before she put the divided nation at risk. Worst of all, she could not hold her own in the shared space with John Williams. That man chilled her to the bone as it was, and if she was off her game she would never be able to stand up against his rhetoric, conspiracies, and bigotry. He was not just a harmless blowhard. He was an ignoramus with power. And if Ann didn't get her act together, she'd be giving him free reign over the entire nation as a whole. So, it was with that attitude that she decided to confront her husband with the truth, all the while knowing it would end her marriage.

But her marriage was already over, she scolded herself. How could she stay with a man who not only cheated, but kept a separate life that involved a child? Maybe even an entire family! *Enough! Go to him, talk. Get this over with. Pull yourself together. You gave up a right to drama in your personal life: You are the President!* Having steeled herself up for the devastation to follow, she entered the great room where Ted was lounging, playing Angry Birds on his iPad. She had gotten him hooked on that silly game and now it felt absurd to end her marriage while talking over the noise of cartoon birds exploding. She stood two feet in front of him, silently waiting. He turned off the iPad.

"Ann, something wrong?" Ted examined her face. Ann said nothing, stayed with her feet rooted into the carpeting. He set down the iPad and stood up, annoying the couple's beloved long-haired cat Greta who had been sleeping with her head on his lap. He walked over to give her a hug but she pushed him away. Greta left the room in a hurry. Startled, he said, "Did *I* do something wrong?"

"Someone is trying to blackmail me with a picture of you with your daughter."

"My *what*?" Ted blinked.

His look of surprise looked genuine. Could it be possible this was a mistake? "Your daughter. The little girl in the picture looks too much like you for me to dismiss the claim as not credible."

"Ann, I'm so sorry you are going through this, but honey, I do not have a daughter. I'm afraid you've been fooled by a Photoshop expert. They probably found a picture of a little girl bearing a resemblance to me and Photoshopped her in, to look like we are in the same shot together."

"I didn't think of that. I want to believe you."

"We can find an expert of our own who can tell us if the picture has been altered, and who can even find the little girl in the picture, find out who she is."

"I need to clear this up, Ted. It's one time I can't take you on your word alone. I'm sorry, but I have to know factually, beyond a shadow of a doubt. You are my world, my best friend. I need to know that I'm not a fool, that I'm not blinded by what I want to believe." Ann's eyes welled up and she forced herself not to lose control.

"I understand, but you'll see. I have never cheated on you, and never will. Tell me more about the picture."

"There was a time stamp on it. It was taken five years ago, so the girl is probably around ten years old now."

"Five years ago? And I had hair, the way it looks now? Ann, that was before I had chemotherapy. You have your proof right there!"

Ann's eyes widened as the light dawned. How could she have missed that? Ted's cancer scare had brought them a year of chemo treatments and fear like no other. At the end of that year Ted was cancer free, but watching his blood count closely for the rest of his life; and he'd also lost all of his hair, which only sparsely grew back. His current sporty "news-anchor-man" do had been created with expensive plugs and faux hair artistry. Prior to his cancer treatments Ted had thicker hair, with a noticeable cowlick. Anyone who knew Ted would instantly recognize his "old" hair. That picture definitely showed off his new hair. She had missed it. She felt wretched.

Ted opened his arms wide. "Come on, bring yourself in." He embraced his wife with all the warmth and strength he could deliver. “I’d never betray you, Ann. We need to find the people responsible for hurting you.”

“I’m sorry I ever doubted you.” Ann sobbed tears of relief, dampening her husband’s shirt with her tears. Much more of this and her nose would be dripping on him too. “How could I have missed the hair?”

Ted gently pushed her away. “Hey, look at me! You are the President! You have the toughest job in the world. I don’t think there’s room left in that big brain of yours to deal with this. Don’t beat yourself up. I’m over it already. You over it? Because I am. Don’t let them hurt you or take your power for a second longer. Fight, honey, don’t let them win.” He drew her back into his chest for another hug.

“I love you,” Ann bawled. She let it all hang out this time, her body racked with all-out crying, her nose and eyes running together into one messy puddle. All the stress of the Office was unloading like a rain shower, soaking the First Gentleman’s shirt.

Ted held her for several long minutes before he abruptly released her. “Ann, you have to pull yourself together. Go clean up. You have a Vid Red.” He jerked his head in the direction of the large flat screen on the wall. A red indicator light was flashing and an electronic warning tone was emitting, easily heard now that Ann had stopped wailing.

Ann was instantly composed, but looked a sight with her red splotchy puffy face and obvious need for a Kleenex. "Turn off the return video feed. Audio only from my end." She dashed to the bathroom to blow her nose and splash water on her face. By the time she returned to the room, the Vid was live.

"I'm here, Breyana. Why are you contacting me with a Vid Red? I expected to see a General's face, not yours."

"Your security detail talked to me. They thought I should do a Vid Red."

"They are there with you?"

"Yes, Madam President," called a voice in the background.

"Step up where I can see you. Tell me what's going on."

"Madam President, we have information about the man you asked us to track."

"Gentlemen, this feed is for national security risks only. Paul is a personal security risk, I made that clear."

"With all due respect, Madam President, we understand the definition of a Vid Red."

"Are you telling me that this man is a national security risk? Even so, a Vid Red means it requires my immediate attention."

"Yes, Madam President. Understood."

Ann exchanged a baffled look with Ted. What on Earth? "You have my attention."

"We have been monitoring his Internet activity. He got an e-mail you need to see."

"Send it through the feed, all windows are open."

Seconds later, this text filled the screen:

>>My Karyn,

I write you heavy heart. You must know for it is my hope you can go safe.

Iran make fools of everyone. For years they lie about nuclear missiles. Nuclear Nonproliferation Treaty is nothing, they spit upon it as easily as they spit on you, dear Karyn.

They threaten who wants make peace with Israel. Pro-West Arab Saudi Arabia and Egypt see Iran success nuclear, but have no fight. Iran pressure Lebanon, Syria, the Palestinians, and the Iraqis. Many thousands, hundred thousands, join radical Islamist. "Death to America!" on Iranian street for too many year. No one stop Iran. Now they make nuclear weapons in short period. They make stockpiles uranium for nuclear device in few months—

make nuclear weapons in short period. They make centrifuges to pipe work. They learn technology when they talk to UN, many lies. Now they can do bomb. They will do this. It will be soon. I hear it from husband. You trust me to know truth. I tell you day and time. I tell you where missiles strike.>>

Ann pointed her finger in the air, swiping the text window off to the right. She stared at the young security officer's face that filled the screen. "What am I looking at? Who forwarded that to him, when, why?"

"The date of the original transmission is the concern."

"I'm sorry, I am not getting any of this. What does Paul have to do with Iran? I am not following this email content."

"The e-mail was originally sent before the Big War, Madam President."

Ann held her hand to her mouth. She remained speechless for several seconds. Ted came up behind her and wrapped his arms around her waist. He whispered in her ear, "You can do this." Then he let his arm slide down to her hand, squeezed her hand, and left her alone to concentrate. She waved at his disappearing back. She turned her attention to the feed. "Who sent this to Paul?"

"Bryce."

"*The* Bryce? John William's Bryce? Be careful now."

"Yes, Madam President."

"I assume you tracked the origin of this e-mail all the way back to the source?"

"Yes, we have. Correct."

"And what did you find?"

"The e-mail has been transmitted many times, Madam President."

"Did it ever reach John Williams' office."

"Yes, Madam President."

"Did it ever reach the President of the United States while he was still in office, prior to the Big War?"

"Yes, Madam President."

CHAPTER 13

Bryce was terribly uncomfortable crunched up in the trunk of Clyde's car. His long lean frame was contorted over a now-full bladder. His mind raced until he hit upon something a former girlfriend once babbled about. What was it she'd said? She saw it on Oprah, or got it in a forwarded e-mail, something like that. It was about if you are ever stuffed into a trunk of a car, what to do. Ah! He remembered. Kick out the taillight. Someone would notice. Hopefully the police.

Bryce kicked and kicked. He had no idea if he was anywhere close to the taillight area, but his foot was hitting on something. He struck out again and again until his heel popped some kind of latch. What was that? Had he popped open the trunk? Yes, the road noise and the rush of air confirmed it. He was free!

He was not bound, gagged, or restrained in any way. Clyde had simply pushed him into the trunk, held him down, and slammed the lid over him. Nothing hurt really, except for his pride. All he needed to do now was climb up and jump out, and hope he could get far enough away before Clyde noticed the trunk lid was open. His opportunity for escape came right away, when Clyde slowed for a four-way stop.

Bryce didn't wait for the car to stop. He hoisted himself up onto his knees, then, as quickly as he could, he climbed out of the trunk and jumped onto the road. He didn't look behind him, but ran on nearly-numb legs, hoping the adrenaline would give him the strength and speed he needed to slip away before Clyde could get to him.

Clyde, confident that Bryce wouldn't be able to get out of the trunk, was unaware of his escape. Not a big fan of defensive driving, Clyde didn't make much use of mirrors or overall attentiveness. His driving time was his down time for personal recreation. He was currently snacking from a new bag of Peanut Butter Bugles while quoting along with "The Notebook". He didn't notice the trunk was open until he parked the car in the garage.

"What's that?" asked Tom.

Paul froze. He could hear Clyde slamming around in the garage, cursing, throwing things. "That would be my brother in a foul mood. I better go see what's going on." As he headed out to the garage, using the door located in the back of the kitchen, Serena returned to the kitchen.

With Paul gone, she could speak freely, but she whispered to be safe: "Tom, he has the e-mail, the one from Karen's friend in Iran."

"The kids are in the car."

"I know, we have to get them out of here."

Tom rose to leave just as Paul and Clyde came in. Clyde snarled, "Where do you think *you're* going?"

"Clyde, calm down, he just finished his coffee. I haven't talked with him yet…" Paul placed himself between Tom and his brother.

Clyde pushed Paul out of the way and grabbed Tom's arm. He pulled him back into the chair. "Toss me some duct tape. It's in the junk drawer."

"I don't think this is—"

"Necessary? Necessary Paul? That's what you were going to say? Well I didn't restrain that idiot Bryce and now he's gone. Won't make that mistake twice. Give me the tape!"

Paul rooted around in the drawer, found the tape, and handed it to Clyde. "There's not much left."

Clyde secured Tom to the chair by wrapping the tape around Tom's middle and the back of the chair, over and over again until the tape was almost gone. He gave Paul the rest of the roll. "Tape his ankles to the chair legs. I'm getting more tape."

As soon as Clyde left the room and Paul was bent over, working on the ankle taping, Serena leaned close to Tom. "Hang in there honey, it will be ok," she said. She tried to give him a meaningful glance but his eyes reflected puzzlement. What was his wife up to? Whatever the secret code was, he didn't get it.

Paul looked up. "Sit down, Serena. You're going to be next."

"I guessed as much. I want to put my chair next to Tom's." She slid her chair near him.

"No, put it back. I don't want you to try to get him out." Paul bent over to work on the second ankle.

"Okay, I'll put it back," she said, and made sliding noises with her chair while slipping her hand under Tom's waistband. Fortunately Clyde's duct tape was above his belly button, nowhere near the handle of the gun. The gun slid out easily. and before she knew it, she was holding a gun, a real loaded gun. If she had time to digest that information she would have been intimidated, but she was reacting on auto-pilot now, feeling nothing, just doing what she needed to do.

Serena held the gun to Paul's head. He looked up at her from his kneeling position near Tom's legs. His eyes registered surprise, but surprise was quickly replaced by mirth. He snickered. "You wouldn't shoot me."

Serena cocked the gun. "I'm Momma Bear and my babies are threatened. You have no idea."

Clyde entered the kitchen from behind Serena, sized up the situation and grabbed a large cast iron skillet. Tom saw him and yelled "Look out!"

Serena whirled around, firing the gun without thinking twice. The bullet hit Clyde's arm. He dropped the skillet. Serena dropped the gun.

Then they both started screaming. Clyde sounded like a wounded animal, Serena hit an octave she normally reserved for when she saw a mouse. The two screamed and screamed, the guttural strangled scream conjoined with the shrill siren scream. The combination shook up the kids in the car.

Carrie called 911. So did a couple of the neighbors. No one knew what was going on, but whatever it was, it sounded like a bloodbath, and then suddenly it was quiet. They thought they heard a gunshot, but weren't sure. The kids were terrified but did not get out of the car. The neighbors locked their doors and stayed away from the windows. Everyone waited for the police to arrive. As they waited, the foursome inside the house took stock of the situation.

Serena broke the silence. She also picked the gun up from the floor and waved it at Paul. "Go stand next to your brother."

Paul didn't move. He looked at her, stunned.

"Now! Go, go! Or I'll shoot you too."

Paul did as she wanted. He moved close to Clyde and stared at his brother's arm. The wound did not look life threatening, but it did look ugly, and painful. Clyde examined it scornfully.

"What's your plan, lady? I bet you don't know what to do now that you've shot me," said Clyde. He spat into the sink from his position a couple feet away. "Do you even know why we have you? We weren't the ones who were going to kill you. They won't care if you've shot me or not. They want me dead too."

Serena looked at Tom. "Paul, I want you to let my husband out. And then he is going to drive our kids somewhere safe."

"I'm not leaving you here, Serena!" said Tom.

"Then let's make this fast so I can go too. Paul, get that tape off of him. Start talking. What did you want with us? Why do you have that e-mail from Iran? How do you know Bryce?" Serena held the gun with both hands. She was struggling to hold her arms steady. She also realized that Paul was not in her line of fire anymore. "Clyde, go stand next to Paul. Go!"

Clyde moved a few steps in that direction.

"Okay, good enough, stay there, don't move." Serena adjusted her stance so that both men were covered by the gun.

Paul took his time cutting the duct tape, stalling. The sooner he freed Tom, the sooner Tom could take over. If there was a reason to shoot, he didn't think Tom would stop at a flesh wound. "I have the e-mail because Bryce sent it to me. He works for President Williams. Williams knew about everything before the Big War. There's a cover up. They want to get rid of anyone who knows about it. You're the target. So am I, and Clyde. We were planning to help you. You shot the wrong guy."

"I don't trust you. What aren't you telling me?" Serena asked, looking from one man to the another.

"What he's not saying is that we planned to give you to Williams to save our own skin. You'd have done the same," said Clyde.

"What about Bryce?" asked Tom. He flexed his ankles, the first part of him that Paul had freed. Paul worked on the duct tape girdle next.

"Bryce escaped. I had him in the trunk. He got out. It's just down to you now," said Clyde.

Paul added, "Now we have nothing. With him gone and you with the gun, we have no leverage. You might as well shoot us -- it would be better than whatever they'll do to me after they put me in prison."

"Would they have killed you anyway, even if you had me and Bryce?" asked Serena.

"We have that e-mail. I've sent it to several safe places," said Clyde. "And we had a plan to record our meeting with them. We'd have enough incriminating evidence to keep us alive. It would have worked. It still can if you play along."

"No thanks. I don't need your plan. You have enough proof with the e-mail. All I have to do is tell the FBI," said Serena.

"That didn't help your friend much, did it?" said Paul. "What protection do you expect from them? William's team found you even when you joined Off Ghost. We're better than witness protection. If we couldn't hide you, they can't."

"I'll go to the top," said Serena.

"He *is* the top," said Clyde.

"You're forgetting about President Kinji. She has just as much power as Williams," said Serena.

"Theoretically," said Clyde with contempt.

"The police are here," said Tom.

"What are you going to do? Press charges? You'll kill us all. William's people will find us," said Paul.

"The police are already at the door," said Serena.

CHAPTER 14

Bryce chuckled to himself. What an idiot Clyde was. He was as stupid as he was ugly. Not only did he not restrain Bryce, but he also didn't think to strip him of his cell phone, which had been on the entire time. Bryce used it now to call his security detail. They could pick him up, no problem. There was a GPS tracker on the phone, which was a good thing since Bryce had no idea where he was, just some country road in the boonies, they all looked the same after a while. He swatted at a deer fly. The sooner he got back to the Windy City the better.

The sound of multiple cars speeding down a nearby gravel road caught his attention. Wow, that was fast. How did they find him already? They must have sent local law enforcement to pick him up. No matter, just as well. He needed a restroom and after that some water, and some food. A good night's sleep sounded good too.

The cars reached him, three government-issue sedans total. It sure looked like secret service detail. But how did they reach him so fast? It had only been about five minutes. Four car doors opened simultaneously: one hulk of a man each from two of the vehicles, and two bureaucratic looking individuals, one male and one female, from the third vehicle.

"Hey guys, how did you get here so fast?" Bryce smiled full wattage, his social smile, not a trace of wolf. He was taken aback when no one responded. One of the beefy men yanked his right arm, another grabbed his left. They steered him toward the nearest sedan. "Hey! What's going on?" Bryce protested. No one answered. "You're taking me to the President? You are, right?"

"Yes, she's waiting for you," said the female bureaucrat.

"She?" Bryce hoped he had heard wrong.

"President Kinji. She's waiting for you. Get in the car."

The convoy, with Bryce pouting in the backseat of one of the sedans, made its way to its next pick-up, about four miles away. Their tires crunched on a long gravel road and then rolled to a stop. Doors opened and shut. The driver of the sedan carrying Bryce did not get out.

"Where are we?" asked Bryce.

The driver looked at Bryce through the mirror but said nothing.

"What is this place?" he tried again.

Still no answer.

"Hey! I know them! What is going on?" Bryce tapped on his window. "Open this up!"

The driver ignored Bryce. Bryce was forced to watch silently from his backseat point of view as four familiar figures were escorted to the other two vehicles. Clyde, his flesh wound bandaged and his arm in a sling, and Paul were led to the sedan behind the vehicle holding Bryce. Serena and Tom, stripped of his gun, which was bagged and tagged, were led to the sedan in front of him. Bryce couldn't hear what they were saying. Completely baffled, he tried to puzzle out what was happening.

Serena spoke to the female bureaucrat, Nancy. "Our kids are still in the car."

"No, they are already with us. They're fine," said Nancy.

"Where are they?" asked Tom.

"We're right here," called Carrie, leaning out the open door of the sleek government vehicle.

"Please get in," said Nancy, gesturing to the generous seating space that her children occupied. Nonetheless, five people made the backseat uncomfortable. No one dared to complain though. After the Meadows were settled in, Nancy shut the door to the backseat, walked to the front passenger's side door, and got in.

"You aren't the police. FBI?" asked Tom.

"No. We are President Kinji's detail," said Nancy.

Her partner Rick started the vehicle and pulled away, leading the convoy of three. "Where are we going?" asked Serena.

Nancy exchanged a look with Rick, who returned her question with a shrug. Nancy hesitated, but then answered Serena's question, "Chicago."

"Chicago!" Serena exclaimed.

"Isn't that a whole day's drive? I need to go to the restroom," said Carrie.

"Do you need to make a rest stop now?" asked Nancy.

"YES!" said the kids and Tom in unison.

"Why are we going to Chicago?" asked Serena.

"President Kinji wants to see you."

"We get to meet the President!" Carrie said. More quietly, addressed to her family, she said, "Had I known, I would have worn something else today."

"Why does she want to see us?" asked Samuel, who had been quiet during all of the excitement. All three kids had kept themselves nearly invisible, but they heard everything that happened within their earshot, and hung on every word. Earbuds or no, when something exciting was happening, they managed to listen.

Nancy shut down the conversation with a firm, "You'll have to ask her that. I am not authorized to brief you. We'll be stopping shortly for a quick restroom break." With that, she pressed the divider button. The Meadows were alone in the backseat, where they quickly took up chatting. The past few harrowing days had renewed their appreciation for each other and suddenly they all had so much to say.

It was far from happy family chatter in the sedan carrying the two brothers. Clyde was seething. "We need a plan," he hissed.

Paul recoiled from Clyde's breath. He couldn't quite define the stench. It was a revolting mix of garlic, coffee, and long-trapped odors from years of plaque build-up, Clyde's own special blend. "I don't know what we can do, Clyde. We might as well hope for the best. At least they aren't taking us to John. Kinji might have a heart and put us in witness relocation."

"Where they will find us and kill us, you know that. At their level, they can ferret out witnesses, protected or not."

"I don't see any solution. I also doubt we're having a private conversation right now."

Clyde snickered. "Of course we aren't, they're listening to everything we say."

"Then I don't know what you expect to plan."

"You're right, we might as well admit defeat," said Clyde. Then he slyly winked at Paul and said, "Just like when we were kids and we were losing at kickball against the Keller kids."

Paul nodded, aware of where Clyde was going with this, and hoping he remembered their secret language. "Yes, who could forget Groin Or Toe Injuries Too?"

Clyde smiled approvingly. Paul did remember: invent a sentence that, when taking the first letter of each word, spells a phrase. Paul had said, "Got it." Just like when they were kids. The code was easier to speak and comprehend with practice, and being brothers, they could practically read each other's minds anyway, so it was easier for them to follow than it would be for most people.

Clyde said, "How Are Children Kickball Enthusiasts? Really Stupid." He felt in his pocket for his cell phone. Yes, there it was, all charged up and everything. Yes, they would know he had used the phone, but it would take them awhile to puzzle out what he used it for. He sent a quick text to one of the kids on his team, the new kid, who wasn't listed on the roster yet. "Activate Clyde. Urgent."

Clyde put his hand behind his back, feigning to massage a painful lower back, while discretely slipping his thumb under the waistband of his jeans until he could feel the elastic band of his briefs. Yes, it was still there: a tiny microphone. Obviously this could be problematic if Clyde had intestinal problems, but it was a good solution to the problem of: what if they forced him to strip down? He figured they were unlikely to make him take off his underwear. He knew Nick would have it up and running before they reached Kinji's office.

"Wacky Happy Youth," said Paul.

Clyde, struggling to come up with a word for each letter, stumbled through the next few sentences at an agonizingly slow pace: "People Let All Youth, Alone. Now Nobody, Just Opens Homes. Neighbors, All Get Annoyed -- Is Never Safe To, Ever Allow Children Home, Outside Their Homes. Everyone's Reality."

Paul traced the beginning letters on his hand until he could piece together what Clyde was saying: *Play Ann, John against each other.* He nodded, ending their tedious conversation. He stared at the divider wall between their seats and the ones occupied by the Muscle. Were they listening? Probably. Paul's mind raced. Clyde's plan was idealistic: he assumed they would be released, free to put the plan in motion. Bring the recordings to both political camps, work a deal.

But Paul had his doubts that either of them would ever be free men. He didn't expect to be alive much longer either. But what was reality to Clyde? Paul's heart sank the more he realized that Clyde had always been crazy, he simply hadn't seen it. He had been caught up in Clyde's plans and schemes for his entire life – could Paul have lived a normal upstanding life had it not been for being raised by an insane brother? Sadly, he would never know the answer. Nor would he have an opportunity to live his life differently.

While Clyde plotted and planned his next move, and Paul sulked, Kinji's surveillance team back in Chicago was cracking up, having figured out the brother's secret code in a matter of seconds. One man laughed so hard that he shot water out of his nose. "We can't make this stuff up," he said, after he recovered.

"I thought they'd break into Klingon," said another.

"Should we send this to Morey in Encrypton?"

"Only if you want your head snapped off."

"Seriously though," said a third, "What do you think they meant by 'play Ann and John against each other'? What are they up to?"

"Doesn't matter," said the first. "They won't be going anywhere."

"It's not like President Kinji is going to waterboard them. There's nothing to hide."

"John has reason to fear a bug."

"Doesn't matter, they won't see him."

"Yes, they will. He'll be there."

"Seriously? What's going down?"

"I don't know. We share the building, it's not that surprising."

"I hope he rots."

"Think these two idiots have something on him?"

"Maybe. If they do, we'll be the first to hear it."

The team continued to monitor the activity in the three sedans, analyzing the feed the mobile team was uploading to them; there wasn't anything else that caught their attention. The Meadow's family was still chatting, but none of what they were saying was of interest to the team. Bryce was silent, as were Tweedle Dee and Tweedle Dum, who the team had dubbed "The Double D's", for Dee and Dum, or "Dumb and Dumber". The rest of the journey went by uneventfully for both the team and the eight passengers they were keeping an ear to.

When the sedans slowed to circle the post-Big-War White House, in the queue to enter the three-mile descent to the underground secured parking area, Serena thought to ask about the third sedan. She had seen Clyde and Paul enter the second vehicle, but what about the third? She knocked on the divider window.

Nancy responded right away with an open window and an invitation, "Yes?"

"Who is in that third car?" asked Serena.

"Not sure you'd know him, but you can see for yourself, he's getting out," said Nancy.

As their own vehicle came to a stop, the other two sedans pulled up alongside them, flanking their car. Paul and Clyde were in the car on their right, so Serena and Tom kept their attention focused on their left, waiting to see who would emerge. They saw the top of his head first, a familiar blond wave, that ridiculous surfer-Prince Charming-frat boy look. Could it be? No, surely not. But it was.

"Why is Bryce here?" asked Serena, panic in her voice.

Nancy's tone revealed nothing. "That's Bryce Otto, one of President William's staff. I don't know why he's here."

"Otto is his last name," muttered Tom.

"Please get out of the car," said the driver of their sedan.

The other two sedans were now empty. The Meadows were slow to get out of the vehicle. "Where are we going?" asked Tom. He and Serena did not move. The three kids looked at their parents for guidance. Rick held the door open for them, but the family didn't budge, unsure of what to do.

"You are not in any trouble, Ma'am, the President just wants to speak with you," said Rick.

"Please come with us now, " said Nancy.

Tom and Serena exited the backseat, taking hold of their children's hands, even though Carrie was a young adult. The five of them looked ready to break into a musical number as they walked hand-in-hand into the White House. It was only after they had been walking down one corridor after another for several minutes that they relaxed enough to release their grip.

The unlikely procession was headed up by Nancy and the Meadows family, followed by Rick escorting Paul, Clyde, and Bryce. The massive drivers of the other two vehicles brought up the rear, sporting ear pieces and ready to tackle anyone who looked at them wrong. They trudged along silently, all of them brooding over what would happen next.

CHAPTER 15

President Ann Kinji waited in her office for the unlikely cast of characters to arrive. She was briefed on each individual and was intrigued by them all. Sensing that at least one of them was certifiably nuts, she requested that a team of psychiatric experts be on hand in the conference room. Each of her guests would have a private meeting in that room before seeing Ann. Those evaluations were now finished and the indicator light on her screen flashed.

Dr. Malik's face appeared in the primary frame. "Madam President, I examined each individual as requested. I found tendencies toward narcissism in both

Bryce Otto and Paul Tracy. Both are also prone to delusional, grandiose visions of themselves."

"Are they dangerous?" Ann asked.

"Not usually, not alone. They are easily manipulated and can be dangerous when paired with someone else who is."

"Is that what we are dealing with here?"

"Yes, quite likely so. Clyde Tracy pulls Paul's puppet strings. Clyde, as we already knew from background investigation reports, has sociopathic behavior. He gave us confirmation, tentative of course without further testing, that he is indeed a sociopath."

"He is dangerous?"

"Yes, probably so."

"And Bryce? Who is his puppeteer?"

"President John Williams, Madam President." There was a long silence that Dr. Malik broke by clearing his throat and adding, "I make no political statement. I am merely reporting my findings."

"I understand."

"Tom and Serena Wilcox and the children are all cleared. We found no reason to suspect mental health issues in any of the five."

"The children? Why are children here?" Ann was alarmed. She'd had no idea that children might be caught up in all of this.

"I don't know the answer to that."

"I want the children moved to a secure location, set them up with pizza and movies, anything they want. Get Breyana on that. Send the others in after President Williams arrives. You can babysit them until then?"

"Yes, of course, Madam President."

"Dr. Malik, thank you and your team for your service. It should go without saying, but this is confidential."

"Of course, Madam President."

"Of course," whispered John from the Listening Room his secret staffers had set up for him. He sounded the alarm. Within minutes he had five covert professionals staring back at him. He didn't know where they came from, or who they were – he didn't need to know. His people handled all of that. Whoever these men were, they operated completely off any records. He wasn't sure they were even fully human.

John's phone lit up. "Yes? No, I'm unavailable. I don't care what you tell her. I was available, and now I'm not."

Breyana brought that message to her boss. "He says he's not available. He's not coming."

Ann felt shivers running down her spine. Something seemed off about this, what could it be? Could he know what was going on? If so, how did he know? She gasped. He was listening. She was sure of it. The more that horrible thought sank in, the more she realized that she never felt alone in her office, even when she was alone. That had to be it. Bugs.

"Madam President?" Breyana looked worried.

Ann scrambled for a pen and paper, hard to find these days, since she seldom wrote anything with real paper. She managed to find a notepad with her Presidential seal on it. She scribbled: "Be careful what you say. Bugs in here."

Breyana's eyes flew open wide. She nodded. "Do you need for me to reschedule your appointments now that President Williams can no longer make it?"

Aloud Ann said, "Yes, please postpone the meetings until the President can make it." Silently, she wrote: "Get them out NOW. Undisclosed location, secret service."

Breyana nodded. Aloud she said, "I'll move those appointments around after I check in with President William's staff." Then she grabbed Ann's notepad and wrote: "You too?"

Ann nodded. "Thank you, Breyana," And because she couldn't resist, and knew he was listening, she added,

"I hope that John isn't ill. I don't know how we'd do without him."

Breyana paused at the door, but Ann waved her to go. It took only ten minutes for Breyana to get the message to the secret service detail, and another ten minutes for the group to be loaded back up in the three sedans.

All passengers were seated comfortably, all but Bryce, who was instructed to lie down in the backseat, even though the windows were tinted, should he be seen through special ops glasses. Hiding Bryce from prying eyes was successful, but the twenty minutes it took to move the group was too long. Deep in the pit of the White House parking catacombs lurked five hulking men.

CHAPTER 16

The five men watched the three vehicles. Everyone was accounted for, and orders were to kill them all. They were ready, and were waiting for the vehicles to start moving. At that moment a fourth sedan pulled up.

"Who is this? You know about this?" grunted one of the hulks.

"Williams said three."

"I don't like surprises."

"What the? There's kids in there. I don't do kids."

As they watched, scopes to their eyes, the Meadows children exited the fourth sedan and climbed into the first sedan in the row, reuniting with their parents. The fourth sedan pulled away, leaving the original three vehicles, but not for long. Two more unexpected sedans pulled up.

"The President is in there!"

"Why is he here?"

"No, not him. The other one."

"Abort. Call John."

The hulks confirmed that John wanted the mission called off. He agreed that it was too complicated now that Ann was involved. He could have sacrificed the kids, but covering up Ann's death would have caused him too many headaches. The investigation into that would have led straight back to him, sooner rather than later.

He'd have to go about this a different way. How? He didn't know. But getting rid of them before they talked to Ann wasn't going to work – his window of eliminating them without a connection to himself had closed.

What did they know anyway? Nothing they could prove, nothing they could tie back to him, and, best of all, their credibility as witnesses was shaky: two con artists, one or both of them mentally unstable, and a family who had been on the run. *Did they have any hard evidence?* He thought not.

John would keep a tail on them and send the team to take them out if necessary – it might not be necessary. If they didn't know anything important, he was trigger happy on this one. He'd find out soon enough when Ann talked about what happened, whether in her office, on her computer, or on her phone – all had John's ears.

The five hulks became phantoms as soon as they confirmed that the mission was aborted; the convoy proceeded unhindered. No one from John's team was following them yet; for the time being they would track them through their phones. With so many cell phones in play, it would be easy to pick up their trail. Meanwhile, they'd let them go for now. The White House underground exits were too vulnerable – a tail would be spotted by many trained eyes.

The convoy reached the last bend of the White House catacombs and then stopped. Nancy and Rick got out of the first sedan. They went to each vehicle and asked for all cell phones, even President Kinji's phone, surprising her with the request. Ann quickly understood and relinquished it.

The last sedan in line carried no passengers. The driver loaded all seven cell phones, including the President's special line, into the trunk of the vehicle. When the convoy reached the end of the catacombs, the last sedan drove in the opposite direction from the other four sedans, carrying their cell phones to an undisclosed location separate, and far away from, President Kinji's undisclosed location destination.

The convoy didn't drive for long- the undisclosed location was Air Force One Plus, Kinji's plane (William's was Air Force One). Air Force One Plus did not share a tarmac with William's plane, and security was tight. Kinji knew that Williams did not have access to her plane, but nonetheless, she had the plane swept for bugs before they boarded. Nothing turned up.

Nor were cameras easy to hijack, but she had her team check and double-check just to be sure. She trusted her people, and after a short security briefing, she felt secure in her choice.

Everyone boarded the plane and waited for something to happen. Two secret service agents guarded the cockpit, others were at the exits. President Ann Kinji remained standing, facing her captive audience. Seated in the front row was the Meadows family. Seated in the second row were Paul, Clyde, Nancy, Rick and Bryce. The remaining rows were used by the rest of the secret service detail.

President Kinji began, "Thank you for putting up with this cloak and dagger routine. Together we'll get to the bottom of this. To start, I'd like to say that I know about the e-mail from the Iranian woman. I also know that the former President and President John Williams knew about the attacks before they happened. What I want from all of you is anything you can add to that."

Serena raised her hand.

"No formalities here, go ahead," Ann said.

"President Kinji, I'm sorry, but I think you know everything that we do. We have only that e-mail." said Serena. She was impressed with herself, how she was able to talk with the President, a woman she greatly admired, as if it were a normal everyday occurrence.

In person, President Ann Kinji was even more amazing. She was beautiful with her shiny black locks and intelligent dark eyes, coupled with a commanding presence and a strong speaking voice. Charisma, confidence and charm were only part of the package; there was a hard-to-define quality that made President Ann Kinji genuine, someone to trust. She was intimidating, and Serena was pleased that she held her own without stammering all over herself.

"But we could get you more," said Paul. "Our plan was to meet with John and record our conversation."

Ann laughed. "Don't you think he'd see that coming?" Her eyes turned up in a smile.

How could she be so jovial and social in such a pressure cooker situation? Serena's respect for Ann went up another notch.

Clyde, however, took offense to the President's amusement. His face flushed crimson and he stood up, causing six secret service officers to also rise. He looked behind him, hesitated for a few tense seconds, and sat back down. He said, "We have high tech ways of recording that can't be detected by bug sweeping."

"Even so, I don't think anything can be gained from that. John wouldn't talk to you, not the truth anyway," said Ann.

"He talked to me!" Paul protested.

Ann's attention was riveted on Paul. "When did he talk to you? Where? What did he say exactly? Leave nothing out." Ann gestured toward two of her staffers who had been standing near the secret service detail in the cockpit. She wanted everything noted, recorded, witnessed. A flurry of activity resulted, followed by silence as all waited for Paul to speak.

Paul glanced around him, suddenly aware that he had the floor. He relaxed, feeling his social grin transforming his face. He might not be doomed after all: *what if Kinji was starting to see him as an asset? Would she toss him aside then?* This was where he was born to be: in the spotlight, important people hanging on his every word.

"Paul, please," said Ann.

"They took me onto his jet, like you've done. He said they 'have ears in Kinj's office'."

Ann blanched at that confirmation of what she already suspected. She had not had her team sweep her office, not wanting Williams to get wind that she knew. "Go on," she prodded.

"He asked how I made that picture, the photo, um, you know the one. I'm sorry about that…"

"I don't care about that right now, keep going."

"He said 'It's good work. I want to use it.' I told him that nobody owns me, but he threatened me."

"Threatened you how?"

"He was going to bug me, follow me, make sure I did what he wanted."

"He likes his bugs. What exactly did he want?"

"He wanted me to bring that photo to the media. He agreed that he wanted to embarrass you and that making trouble for you keeps you off balance."

President Ann Kinji drew up her full height and took a deep steadying breath. All of her martial arts training came back to her. She felt her body go into "ready position" even while appearing outwardly to not move a muscle. "So far this is nothing more than dirty politics, smear campaigns, intimidation. Same-o, same-o. I need proof that John knew something about the Big War."

Clyde said, "He broke the law, you could get him for that. And then interrogate him."

"I don't think I could get anywhere with nothing but the word of a known con man," said Ann.

"Don't take my word for it, get his records. He has a folder with everything in it, even references to the Academy and good old Mrs. Mason, may she rest in peace," said Clyde.

Ann took notice. "What records?"

"He, um, wanted to talk about my, as he put it, 'fear mongering' about the Identity Chip bill, the reason why I wanted to work for you, why I brought that doctored photo to you for leverage," said Paul.

"You would have never been able to leverage me, but go on," said Ann.

"I wanted to work for you so that I could influence that Identity Chip bill. I wanted it to pass so that people would buy Clyde's Angels Mark technology," said Paul.

"You're losing me, what does anything of this have to do with records?" asked Ann.

"I'm getting to that. He said, 'you didn't think I knew all about your operation?' And told me 'my guys briefed me about your whole life in fifteen minutes. It's all right here.' He had a brown folder."

Ann laughed, "No! He wouldn't have anything on paper. You expect me to believe he had a brown folder!"

Paul protested, "He did! He even said, 'I could read it on one of those gadgets, but I like paper.' He said he *likes* paper. He has a paper trail. We can find it."

Ann's hopes were raised, but she didn't want to get too excited. "Hmm, I'm not convinced."

Paul said, "He said that someone would pay me, and the money in my account would be, and I quote, 'Untraceable to this office'. But I know that Clyde's lab could crack whatever code they have."

"Clyde's lab of child hackers? This isn't going anywhere," said Ann. She sighed.

"Wait, wait!" Paul said. "*He* was there!" He pointed at Bryce. "He heard everything, and he works for John."

"Bryce was there?" Ann smiled. "Interesting. We'll be getting to Bryce, but have you told me everything you know? Everything John told you? Everything you saw?"

Paul shook his head slowly from side to side, like a small boy interacting with his kindergarten teacher. "I can't think of anything else."

"Okay then, what we've got so far is the possibility that President Williams has paper records that may or may not incriminate him. I hope Bryce can offer us something more substantial than that," said Ann.

All eyes were on Bryce. He said, "What makes you think I would tell you anything? He's not only my uncle, he's my President."

President Kinji glared at him and took a few steps toward where he was sitting. She said, "One word: *treason.*"

Bryce made a dramatic *ppft* sound and said, "How can it be treason to protect my President? That's the epitome of loyalty, not grounds for treason."

"Your loyalty is to your country, and your people, not to any one President. You knew about this e-mail—you are the very person who shared it. You knew that President Williams was involved in acts against our country, and you said nothing. You even perpetuated this massive cover-up, and whatever it is that John is trying to do," said Ann in a quiet, controlled, voice. Slow, steady, and smooth, like talking to a rabid dog.

Bryce tried a new tactic, "How do you know that the e-mail isn't a fabrication?"

Serena interjected, "I know it isn't. My friend Karyn is the original recipient of that e-mail. I saw it on her computer, and I even have the flash drive with the entire history of her correspondence with Farideh on it." She waved her flash drive, jingling the crowded key ring that the flash drive keychain was attached to.

Ann said, "I was going to get to you next, Serena, but I'm going to go straight to you right now." She clucked her tongue, her eyes turning up at the corners to match her grin. "Amazing, you have something we can actually use. Oh most definitely!" She clapped her hands together and said, "Nance, take that flash drive from her, would you please? Get everything off of it. *Now* we're getting somewhere!"

"Uh oh, I'm afraid that's really all I have," said Serena. "Although I did have a thought. We knew back in 2011, when the Iranians shot down our spy plane, that Iran was getting close to having the technology to make weapon-grade uranium for nuclear weapons."

"Yes, Tehran's nuclear program, the Fordo uranium enrichment site. What's the connection to John?" Ann said.

"Well, obviously some of their actions since then led to the Big War, and there would be records of those actions. I am thinking that John may have been deeply involved in those talks. Maybe you can follow that all the way up to the days leading up to the bombings," Serena offered.

Ann frowned. "I don't think those records would be revealing. Anything sinister would have taken place outside of recorded meetings. I need John's personal files, and I want you to get them, Bryce."

"Even if I wanted to help you," said Bryce, "I can't get to his files without being seen. I mean, if people saw me, they wouldn't think twice, but I'd leave an identity mark that would sound off an alarm. No one but Uncle John, uh, President Williams, can authorize or access his office or computer. They'd have those files from me before any of you ever saw them."

"Are you sure about that? I have an idea," said Serena.

"Yes? Listening," said Ann.

Tom looked at his wife. *What idea did she have?* After all these years, he still couldn't tap into her head.

No one else on the plane could guess either, and all strained their ears to hear what she had to say.

"I thought of it when Paul mentioned the Identity Chip. President Williams uses it already doesn't he? I remembered that I saw on the news that his entire wing of the White House switched over to that system, sort of a demo, showing how the IC works," said Serena.

"Yes, they've been using it for months now, garnering support for the IC bill by showing off its success," said Ann. "Where are you going with this?"

Serena turned around in her seat to look directly into Clyde's rheumy eyes. "Is your Angels Mark technology for real, or is that part a scam too?"

Clyde made a show of being offended, but he was gearing up for a grand-standing moment. "Yes, it's for real! We would have made millions off of it."

Paul chimed in, "Did you think our grand plan was to minister a mega church forever? I had those people wanting the Angels Mark technology even before its release."

Clyde, getting revved up, said, "It's all in the marketing. You know your market, you feed into their fears, their paranoia, their delusions, then give them what they want: something to make the evil go away."

"I can't believe people are so easily led, " Ann argued.

"We'd have gotten the entire flock of sheep, we'd have cornered the Christian-right market!" Clyde snarled, spittle frothing in the corners of his mouth. "You don't know what you are talking about."

Paul added, calmly, "It's moved out of beta. It works. We were ready to roll it out whenever the IC bill passed."

Ann said, "You've lost me. What is Angels Mark?"

Serena, Paul and Clyde all started talking at once, and it was only when young Samuel spoke up that everyone stopped the race to be the spokesperson for defining the Angels Mark.

President Kinji gave the nod to Samuel. "If you can explain it to me, I'd appreciate it," she smiled.

Samuel's passion for computers bubbled over and his words tumbled out of his mouth quickly, his conversation difficult to follow. "Angels Mark is software that can override the system of the Identity Chip. They can program whatever they want in it and the system of the IC will think it's the right code when it's really any code that they want. They call it Angels Mark because they say that the IC is the mark of the beast, from Revelations, but I don't believe that, I think they made that part up, not that Revelations is what they made up, they made up the part about the chip being from that. They say the beast is a computer, not a person, and his mark is the IC, which I don't believe at all, they can't fool me. But if you get the chip and get the Angels Mark it's like not taking the number of the beast because they can change the number to anything they want and the IC is overridden…"

"Wow, thank you, young man, whew!" Ann cut him off, realizing that the child would keep going for as long as she allowed him to ramble. "So, if I'm getting this right, we can use this Angels Mark software to erase Bryce's security breach? Use his well-known face to get him into the office with no problems; then erase what he's doing in there? Correct?"

"Yes," said Serena.

"Technically, I'm not sure they can erase the fingerprint, they might need to substitute John's code for Bryce's. I'll have to leave that up to the crew to determine," said Clyde.

Ann waved that off. "Doesn't matter. We can get the files, can we not? It can be done?"

Paul and Clyde said in unison, "Yes."

Everyone looked at Bryce.

"What happens to me? Do I get a deal?" he asked.

"So much for loyalty to Uncle John," said Ann.

"When you guys get through with him he won't be able to help me. I'm not going down with him when he tanks, he'd do the same if he were me, do you think he wouldn't bail on me? But before I switch teams I want a guarantee: Lawyer, papers, signed by a judge. I want it in writing, I repeat, signed by a judge," said Bryce.

"You've got it," said Ann, her voice dripping with disgust. She stood for a few seconds, lost in thought. "Oh, I do have one more issue to bring up. Serena, your friends

Karyn and Dan have been moved to a safe house. She asked me to be sure to tell you."

Serena felt a twinge of discomfort upon her conscience, realizing that she hadn't stopped to think about what had happened to her good friend Karyn. She was relieved to hear that she was okay. "Thank you for letting me know," she said.

And with that, the meeting was adjourned. President Kinji's staff flew into action, and the pilots were brought on board. Everyone was instructed to buckle up to prepare for their flight to Minneapolis, a city they'd seen more of lately than usual. As a result, the media was starting to make some noise, speculating about why President Kinji had stepped up the frequency of her trips there. Even though her trips were not made public, the world always knew of her whereabouts eventually.

Once in the air, and after the plane leveled out to a smooth steady plateau in the sky, Serena and Tom held a private conversation that was only partially overheard by their children, and went no further.

"Tom, I feel so humiliated by this Angels Mark nonsense," said Serena.

"What do you mean?"

"To be caught up with those deranged brothers, it's awkward. Their scam is so icky, preying on religious people. They are twisting things that people really do believe passionately in."

"We weren't taken in by it."

"I know, but we are not as gullible as some. Even so, it's embarrassing to be connected to this. I really admire President Kinji," Serena said, barely above a whisper. "All that stuff about the Beast, she probably thinks we're crazy by association."

"No, I'm sure she doesn't. Besides, Angels Mark is a real technology they invented, if it works."

"I think it will. I don't trust the Tracy brothers, but I do trust those kids in the computer lab," said Serena.

The two continued to talk in hushed tones, and when they had finally exhausted all topics relating to anything important, their conversation drifted to what their plans might be for dinner.

Meanwhile, President William's covert detail was following the decoy sedan, with its decoy convoy, all the way to Newton, Kansas. The lead driver, relieved of his Chicago duty, was hurrying home to his wife, a petite brunette named Kelly who was cooking his favorite farm-raised beef in her often-used crock pot.

It would be a long night for the covert team, smelling a supper they couldn't have, hearing the sounds of TV and laughter, and eventually blinking in the darkness; finally admitting to themselves and to each other that they had been had.

No one wanted to report their failure to Chicago, but one unlucky member of the team drew the short straw. President Williams needed to know: they'd been had. And none of them had the slightest idea where Madam President or her odd cast of cohorts was. The unlucky short-straw bearer held his earpiece away from his ear as Williams bellowed, ranted, and cursed until he ended the call.

CHAPTER 17

As William's five men watched the three vehicles, one of them reported back that everyone was accounted for. The response: Orders are to leave no witnesses. All eyes were trained on the targets; two of the less fortunate assassins were assigned to keep their scopes on the most volatile and least physically attractive witness Clyde Tracy.

Clyde hugged himself tightly, as close as he would ever get to being embraced by another person. This was the highlight of his entire life: the fate of the world was up to Clyde. He had always known that this was his destiny.

Everything he had ever done in his life was worth it, for this very moment, one of few moments he had left here on this earth. He would have done it all over again.

Clyde was with President Kinji's new covert A Team, to oversee the install of Angels Mark and the re-insertion of the modified Identity Chip under Bryce's skin. He watched the testing of the chip, and gave it his approval. He nodded authoritatively toward President Kinji's secret service agents. The procedure was complete. He looked with satisfaction at his lab, newly staffed with government suits, buddied up with his teenage hackers: how else could they be brought up to speed on everything so quickly? These kids were having the time of their lives, just as Clyde was. The mood in the lab was buoyant to say the least.

Nancy and Rick were taking lead on the Angels Mark project. Rick said, "We'll be bringing Bryce back to Chicago now."

"What about me, about us?" said Paul.

"No, we won't be needing you," said Rick.

"Yes you will," fumed Clyde. "You need someone to analyze the data."

"We have people who will analyze it. You're staying here," said Nancy.

"You can't take my technology and leave me behind," said Clyde.

"Someone will be in touch," said Nancy curtly. She spun on her heels and took Bryce by the arm. Rick took up his other arm. They half-dragged him out of the building even though Bryce was leaving willingly.

"Wait, wait!" called Bryce. The two agents ignored him, so Bryce kept talking, shouting over his shoulder, while Clyde and Paul followed him out the door to catch his every word. "Gustavo, the general, he's sympathetic to your cause. Talk to him!"

Bryce was pushed into yet another government vehicle and rushed to a secret runway where a small jet was waiting to return him to the White House.

The two brothers went back into the computer lab; Bryce's parting comments weighing on their minds. Clyde asked Paul, "Where's that detective lady?"

"Who?"

"Serena what's-her-name."

"She's a detective?"

"She used to be."

"What do you want her for?"

"My lab is tied up, my hackers are tied up, and besides, they're watching us."

"You want her to find the general?"

"They said they don't need us. We'll see," said Clyde defiantly.

"She went home with the rest of her clan. But there's security on them."

"We aren't going to scare her. No reason for security to have their panties in a bunch. Let's pay her a visit."

The farmhouse the Meadows family was resting comfortably in was only a few miles from the lab. In less than ten minutes Paul and Clyde were at her doorstep, where they were greeted with suspicion by two secret service agents.

"What are you doing here?" asked the one with carroty red hair, hair that was impressively fluorescent even while diminished somewhat by his crew cut.

"We just want to talk with Serena," said Paul.

The second agent, a black male who stood an impressive six feet nine inches at his full height, was stooped over to fit under the standard-sized door frame. "You can talk to her from here."

Serena heard the conversation and came closer. "What do you want?"

"We got a tip that General Gustavo is willing to work with us, but we need help in finding where he is. President Kinji's team is using the lab," said Paul.

"Gustavo…Wasn't he interviewed a few years ago, before the Big War, back when the national debt ceiling crashed?" Serena shut the screen door before unidentified biting bugs made their way into the house.

"I don't know, maybe," said Clyde, who hadn't flinched when the door was shut almost in his face.

"Yes, I remember," said Paul. "He was part of a press conference, about our readiness to go to war. It was right after the markets seized up and the U.S. caused the world economy to crash."

"The default had a catastrophic effect on financial markets. We made a lot of enemies. I can remember a little of Gustavo's speech now," said Serena.

"What difference does this make?" asked Clyde.

"Maybe none. Why are you here?" asked Serena.

"We told you that already. We got a tip."

"From who?" asked Serena.

"Bryce. From Bryce. Look, we need your help in finding the General. The lab is all tied up with Kinji's people. You're supposed to be a detective, or at least you were. Can you find where he is?" asked Paul.

"Does President Kinji know about this?" asked Serena.

"She's the one who wants us to talk to him," Paul lied.

"She didn't contact me," said Serena.

"She went back to the White House, when they brought Bryce back," said Paul, which was the truth.

Clyde, sensing she needed more verification of Kinji's involvement, appealed to her ego, "President Kinji said that you'd be able to find him, no problem. Was she wrong?"

Serena blushed at the idea of President Kinji recommending her specifically. "I don't know if I can find him, but I can try. Come in."

Clyde flashed a leering grin at the two agents as he walked past them. *The puppet master hasn't lost his touch!* He and Paul joined Serena and Tom at their kitchen table, where they sat for a good hour before Serena found what she was looking for.

"I had to pay one of those services to dig a little deeper than what I could find for free, but I finally found a home address for him. You didn't tell me he had a residence in Minnetonka. That's what, less than two hours' drive?"

Paul and Clyde registered genuine surprise on their faces. "We didn't know he was so close," said Paul.

"You're going to go talk to him?" asked Tom.

"Yes," said Paul.

"Did she want us to come with you?" asked Serena.

The brothers hesitated, working through the pros and cons quickly. On one hand, they wanted all the glory of the mission. On the other hand, they could use some help. Serena might be the better conversationalist, especially if the general wasn't home, and only his wife was available. "Yes, she assumed you'd be coming with us," said Paul, looking at Clyde for validation, and receiving it with a slight nod, that he made the right decision.

"We need to go right away," said Clyde. He looked back through the kitchen into the living room at where the kids were working on various projects. "This time, leave the kids at home."

"Good point. You'll be fine, won't you? The agents will be here," said Serena.

"Yes," the three kids said, nearly in unison. By now they were unflappable.

The red-headed agent stopped them as they headed out. "We're supposed to stay with you."

"We'll be right back, please keep an eye on the kids," said Serena.

"We are not babysitters, ma'am."

"Isn't the detail assigned to the house?" asked Tom.

The red-head answered, "I'll go with you. Special Agent Thompson will stay here."

Clyde and Paul went together in Clyde's vehicle. Tom and Serena rode with the red-head who introduced himself as Special Agent Salisbury. With the team of Thompson and Salisbury split up, neither man had backup, but given the egos of both agents, neither one thought twice about breaking protocol.

The journey to General Gustavo's home felt long. It had been a draining twenty-four hours. And now it was getting dark. It was hard for Tom and Serena to keep their eyes open. Fortunately neither of them was driving.

The two vehicles, Clyde's jeep and Salisbury's government issue, pulled up alongside the front entry of the house, a modest home in a nice suburban neighborhood. The four of them lagged behind while Salisbury led the way, as he insisted upon doing.

Before Salisbury could ring the bell, the door was opened by General Gustavo himself. "Identify yourself, Agent."

"Special Agent Salisbury, Sir."

"Where's your partner?"

"He stayed back on detail."

"Come in." General Gustavo ushered them all inside. "We can talk in the den." He led them down to the finished basement level, to the farthest room from the stairs, a room with no windows. "Please secure the room, Agent."

"Sir? Secure the room?" Salisbury was confused. Why would the general need his home office swept? Wouldn't he know if there was someone lurking in there? But his legs carried him into the room as ordered.

Gustavo promptly shot him in the back. It made little sound. The thud of Salisbury's body as it fell to the floor seemed louder. Blood pooled around him as the four visitors stared at his prone body, his trademark red hair now made a dark crimson. It seemed like blood was everywhere.

Salisbury must have hit his head on something on the way down to account for all that blood, thought Serena. *We're all going to die.* She began to pray.

"Bryce!" yelled Clyde.

General Gustavo grinned. "It was a nicely set trap. The President wants you out of the way. But not until you tell me what Kinji knows."

"If you're going to kill us anyway, why should we tell you anything?" asked Serena.

Tom did not have his gun with him; the secret service had not returned it. He looked around him for a means of escape. He could find none. He kept looking.

Paul looked at Clyde with despair; Clyde's arm was still in a sling and neither of them had a weapon. He said, "Make us a deal and we'll tell you want you want."

"I don't make deals. I'll pick you off one by one until you talk." Gustavo snorted like a bull. "Starting with *you.*"

Gustavo pointed the gun directly at Paul's head. Seeing his brother in danger triggered something primal in Clyde. Unhindered by the sling, and feeling no emotion, no pain, Clyde charged at Gustavo, screaming a most unholy shriek as he lunged.

The attack was so quick, so unexpected, and accompanied by such a surprisingly hideous sound, that Gustavo was caught off guard. Clyde was at this throat, with both of his hands, the arm sling twisting under pressure, as he grasped hold of Gustavo's neck, strangling him with his bare hands.

Gustavo's eyes bulged and he managed to squeeze off a round, but he was no match for Clyde's insanity. He was limp and lifeless without ever uttering another syllable.

Gustavo dropped to the floor, immediately followed by Clyde himself. That one round, that the general had fired off while in the throes of death, had hit Clyde at extremely close range, a fatal wound, which was now obvious to the remaining three witnesses to the past few seconds. No one moved at first, and then Paul rushed to Clyde's side.

"Nooooo! Nooooo!" Paul wailed. He held his brother's head in his lap, staring down in horror as blood frothed from Clyde's mouth. "Quick, Serena! You believe for real, right? My brother deserves last rites."

Serena stammered, "I'm not a clergy. I'm not sure what you want—"

"Pray! He's dying! My brother is dying!" Paul sobbed.

Serena didn't know how to pray for the soul of a man like Clyde, so she recited the Lord's Prayer from memory:

"Our Father, who art in Heaven, hallowed be thy name, thy Kingdom come, thy will be done, on Earth as it is in Heaven…"

The mention of Heaven caused a great outburst from Paul, who was now soaked in his brother's blood. He clutched at Clyde's shirt, grabbing him into a floppy, unresponsive embrace.

Serena let her words trail off and tried to look away from the macabre sight, but a mixture of horror and fascination kept her eyes rooted to the two brothers. Seeing the blood pooling on the floor, and all over Paul, and the blood spatter from Gustavo all over the walls, furniture, and floor, she studied her new green trench coat with its trendy styling and chic belt for signs of crimson:

whew, no blood stains. She glanced at Tom, who was turning quite pale and looked ready to faint.

Paul began rocking from side to side, holding his brother's body and wailing. While Paul was consumed and distracted, Serena and Tom took the opportunity to slip out of the room. They called 911, then President Kinji at the special number she gave them.

CHAPTER 18

While Bryce's trap was ensnaring Clyde, and General Gustavo as collateral damage, Bryce was dutifully playing for the other side. He slipped into President John Williams' private office areas without raising any suspicion whatsoever, which was as he expected. The tricky part would be to access and copy his uncle's files without his fingerprints setting off any alarms. He hoped the Angels Mark worked. He couldn't care less about helping Ann; he did care immensely about being caught helping her. He had every reason to have a healthy fear of how far John would go if he knew that Bryce was selling him out. He feared John much more than he feared prison, but he preferred to avoid both. If this Angels Mark technology worked, he would extract the files with no one the wiser.

He held his breath as the download indicator bar filled. The transfer speed was the best there was, and Bryce was soon out of his misery. No alarms. Nothing. He had done it! He worked his way through every folder, including those that were hidden. He himself had organized most of these, so he knew where the secret files were. At this point, he was all in and wanted as much incriminating evidence as possible to get protection for himself from John. He figured the only chance he had was if they branded John as not only a traitor, but the world's most wanted terrorist. If they got all of John's people too, Bryce had a fighting chance of hiding away somewhere and starting a new life. He copied everything he could find, even files he didn't think were important.

Just as he finished copying the files, Bryce's heart stopped beating. President John Williams, his revered and feared uncle, was standing in the entrance to his private office area. "Hey, Brycer! What are you doing in here?"

A practiced liar after years of picking up girls and lying to his parents about his whereabouts, it was natural for Bryce to concoct a plausible story on the spot. "I was hoping to check my e-mail. The battery on my phone is dead."

"What's wrong with your office?" John asked. Not suspicious, not judging, just a simple question an uncle might ask his nephew.

"I'm avoiding Caroline," he said, which was partially true, actually. He had slept with Caroline a few times, and now she expected a ring. That was never going to happen, especially now.

John chuckled. "Understood."

Bryce smiled full wattage, a ladies' man just like his uncle, the good old boys' club, partners, on the same team. "You have a full plate today. How are you going to fix this thing with Kinji?"

"Oh don't worry about that, I have my people on it. By this time tomorrow, she won't be a problem," said John ominously.

Bryce shuddered inwardly. *Better her than me*, he thought. Relieved that he had gotten away with betraying his uncle in plain sight, Bryce slipped down the corridor and left the White House for a restaurant well known as a spot for politicians to gather. No one would think twice about Bryce being there, or seeing him meet up casually with someone from Kinji's staff, placing his flash drive into the palm of Breyana's pretty little hand.

Back at the White House, President Ann Kinji waited anxiously for Breyana to return. She had no fewer than seven secret service agents with her, so surely Breyana would be safe. However, after hearing the disturbing news about General Gustavo and Clyde, she had every reason to worry. She feared that Bryce was laying down another trap, but then again, she banked on Bryce wanting to save himself.

She wondered if John even knew yet that things had gone wrong. Was Gustavo instructed to merely hold them, not kill them? Obviously John wouldn't have thought that the general would get killed. When Ann had spoken to Bryce, Bryce had the attitude of someone who had finished a mission, cocky, relaxed. She didn't think that he knew that Gustavo was dead. And if not, how could that be? Wouldn't John be expecting Gustavo to report in regularly? Either John didn't know what happened, or he didn't trust Bryce anymore. The first scenario worked well in their favor, the second one was chilling.

"Bird is in the cage," said Special Agent Smith in her ear.

"Thank you, Special Agent Smith. No problems?"

"No, Madam President. She'll be with you shortly."

"Thank you, thank you!" Ann breathed a sigh of relief. Breyana was young, with her whole life ahead of her.

Putting her in danger was wrong. But Breyana had volunteered, and in the end, Ann couldn't think of anyone else she trusted to make the exchange. With great reluctance, and a whole swat team of agents, Ann had let her go. And here she was!

"I got it," sang Breyana. She extended her arm, opened the fingers that had been gripping the flash drive tightly for the past fifteen minutes, and showed her boss the smoking gun: a small shiny gadget that held who knew what.

"Oh, thank you, Breyana, I sure could use a cup of coffee," said Ann.

Breyana froze, a puzzled expression on her face, until Ann put her index finger to her lips, then pointed to the general direction of President William's office and cupped her ear. Breyana nodded. "No problem."

"I think I'll take my coffee on the way out the door. I have a meeting with the governor of Indiana this afternoon."

"Should I let them know you're ready to go?" asked Breyana.

"Yes, please do," said Ann.

Within the hour Ann was seated once again on Air Force One Plus. The computers were safe here on the plane, transmitting on channels that were tracked by more agencies than John would have been able to corrupt. Her hunch was that if her phones were tapped, her office bugged, well, naturally John had his dirty fingers all over her computer. She didn't dare open those files until she was on a secure connection. But here she was, in a safe place, on a safe connection, with people who would keep her, and the information she held, safe. As much as she dreaded seeing the truth laid out in black and white, it was time for the big reveal.

The first thing Ann did was copy all of the files and send them to multiple places. Next, she asked one of her IT agents to put what she was seeing up on multiple screens. "Thank you, Agent Lehman. I'm ready now; please tell them to come in."

Serena and Tom entered the plane, still traumatized by the day's events, but in enough shock that nothing felt real. After Serena had phoned President Kinji, right after Clyde's horrific and revolting demise, a team of agents was quickly on the scene at the house in Minnetonka, where Gustavo had never actually lived – funny how fabricated records can appear instantly in the right places when powerful people want them there.

The agents had whisked them out of the house, some staying behind to clean up the mess, and taken them to yet another secret airstrip. This one appeared to be in use by hobbyists, but it was available at that moment for a government jet – off record.

Once again, Serena and Tom were flown into Chicago, but this time they left their children in the safe keeping of Special Agent Thompson- who was beginning to think of himself as an over-muscled nanny- and two more agents who had been assigned to replace the ill-fated Special Agent Salisbury.

"I'm so sorry for what you've been through," Ann began. "I want you to know that your country, that I, appreciate all you've done."

"Thank you, President Kinji," said Serena.

"No problem," said Tom, which elicited a look of disbelief from both Ann and Serena.

"I hate to ask more of you, and I'll be sure that you are both generously compensated, but I trust the two of you as witnesses, and well, you are already involved. I want you to read this material along with me. I have sent the material to several sources, but it will go unread until I give the word. I have also asked my husband, Ted, to sit in with us," Ann gestured toward the seats behind them.

Ted stood up and shook their hands. No one spoke. The three stood for a few awkward seconds. Ann broke the tension, "Sit, we are ready. Look at the screen nearest you." She took a deep breath. "Here we go."

Ann clicked through twenty five folders, each containing over a hundred individual files. She skimmed through the first folder, with everyone watching on the various screens, and then realized that it was going to take a lot more time than she expected to wade through all the trivial saved documents to find the incriminating evidence.

She instructed Special Agent Lehman to set up shop for Ted, Tom and Serena to work through files on three more stations. Her request was quickly granted. For the next four hours, the four of them pored methodically through every folder and file, each person with their own section, so as not to miss a single document. Finally, it was Ted who signaled he found something by whistling softly through his teeth.

"I think you better put this up to share on all screens," he said. Special Agent Lehman scurried to comply. And there is was; one of several guns that were smoking big black billows of toxic, toxic air.

<<I do not recommend reliance upon the MDS /Missile Defense System/ as a means to protect the nation from the imminent nuclear attack /CLOSED DOCUMENT: 2 authorized>>

<</PAGE 2/You continue to rely upon the MDS against my recommendation. Insubordination not withstanding, what the hell is going on?>>

"What are we looking at? Who is this, and is it the same person in both messages?" asked Ann.

"Yes, same source," said Special Agent Lehman.

"If I were to guess, the general?" said Tom.

"Makes sense," said Ann. "Move on."

Ted clicked on the next message:

<<Think of a nation without debt, without reliance upon foreign oil. Think of starting over, closed borders. Think of our economy – restored /CLOSED DOCUMENT: 3 authorized>>

<<You are saying that we let them bomb us? Who did you CC, I have you and the Pres only/CLOSED DOCUMENT: 2 authorized>>

<<You, me, the President – that's 3. How did you do your math/CLOSED DOCUMENT: 3 authorized>>

<<Sorry, Big W, I forgot to CC myself/CLOSED DOCUMENT: 3 authorized>>

Serena said, "President John Williams is well known as 'Big W'. This should work toward proof of his involvement."

"I think we can get more solid proof by tracing these messages back to their digital fingerprint, am I right?" asked Ann.

"Yes, Madam President, exactly," said Special Agent Lehman.

"There's more in the next folder," said Ted. He opened the next series of messages:

<<Before I agree to recommend the MDS plan, I need it from you President. No offense, John, but I need a reason before I agree to let them drop nukes on our own people/CLOSED DOCUMENT: 3 authorized>>

<<Bipartisan government, deadlocked, economy in the sewer, lobbyist in all of our pockets, oil so high we can't pay it, borders so open we can't keep them out. Bigger and bigger we get, resources smaller and smaller. No plague to shrink us, no war to eradicate us. Can't stop this mutating nation from self-destructing. This is our plague: we can start over. I will step down, give the nation a rebirth./CLOSED DOCUMENT: 3 authorized>>

<<This doesn't sound like a Democrat/CLOSED DOCUMENT: 3 authorized>>

<<John, why would we want this chaos? We will never agree to the Republican view, but we've come together on this: we must destroy ourselves to fix what's broken. Satisfied, General?/CLOSED DOCUMENT: 3 authorized>>

<<I want you to confirm in person with your own two lips that this is what you want, and if it is, I will do what you ask/CLOSED DOCUMENT: 3 authorized>>

"Wow, this is hard to believe," said Serena.

"Is there more, Ted?" asked Ann.

"Do we really need more?" asked Ted. "Let the law take it from here. You don't need to be personally investigating this."

"I have to agree with the First Gentleman, Madam President, let us get all the agencies on this," said Special Agent Lehman.

"May I suggest that you stay out of the White House for a while? Whatever happens next shouldn't touch you or your Presidency," Serena volunteered. She patted herself on the back for how much she sounded like an official advisor to Madam President.

"Back to Minneapolis? Reunite you with your family?" Ted suggested.

"I can't get used to Minneapolis being the place to be," said Tom.

"The new Wall Street, the Pentagon, the split Capital building. Brings us in," said Ted.

"But why Minneapolis? Why are they rebuilding the Pentagon in Minneapolis and not Chicago near the White House? And why have two Capital buildings?" asked Tom.

"After 9-11, some questioned the wisdom of us having all of our governmental buildings in one basket. Spreading ourselves out, with the full capacity to govern out of two separate cities seemed wise, given that we'll never fully be rid of the threat of terrorist attacks," said Ann.

"And look at us now, needing to leave Chicago. It's good to have a secondary location," said Ted.

"I know of a farmhouse where you could wait for the green light to go back to Chicago," said Serena.

Would it be too much to ask to have the President to her house for coffee and a girlfriend chat? No matter how wretched the day's events were, it was hard not to feel a thrill at the thought of entertaining President Ann Kinji in her home.

"I haven't been in a real house in years. I'll take you up on that offer," Ann said.

Serena resisted the urge to squeal with glee.

CHAPTER 19

Paul obediently followed the agents out of the house in Minnetonka. He struggled through that first hour in a daze, not knowing how to formulate a single thought. How could he exist without Clyde? He stumbled down the sidewalk and allowed himself to be tucked into a government vehicle.

As he sank into the leather seat his heart welled up with fury and grief. The longer he sat, the more his grief was channeled into fury. President John Williams, and the previous President, pre-Big War, pre-apocalypse, had killed his brother. Paul was no sociopath, but Clyde had killed for him, and had ultimately died for him. It was the least Paul could do to avenge his brother's death.

He knew that John would be taken care of; he'd be tried as a traitor, a terrorist. The divided nation would turn on him and curse him to the end of his days. But the former Prez? What of him? Had Kinji even put two and two together yet? Paul wasn't so sure. And how deep was the cover-up? Would John take the Prez's involvement with him to his grave?

The thought of him getting away with it, with Clyde's blood on his hands, made Paul's blood boil. The only thing on his mind was finding the former president of what was once the United States of America.

The agents dropped him off at home. They informed him that he would be contacted shortly, to be interviewed for a criminal investigation into President John Williams' conduct before and after the Big War. Then they left him alone, re-assigned elsewhere. Apparently no one considered broken down wanna-be Paul to be a threat.

Paul locked the door and latched the dead-bolt. He went into the laundry room and took off his blood-drenched clothes. He hesitated, not knowing what to do. He had never done a load of laundry in his life. Where did the detergent go? Did he put it in now or after the clothes were in? Should he even bother – would the blood stains come out? He lifted the lid of the washer and, much to his surprise, saw directions for how to use the machines right there on the lid. He followed the instructions on the chart and started the washer.

Then he shuffled his way to the bathroom to take a shower. He did a double-take at his reflection in the mirror: was that Clyde's face staring back at him? He closed his eyes; then opened them again. No, he saw his own face. He couldn't tell if he was relieved or disappointed. He would never see his brother's face again: he didn't have a single picture of Clyde, unless he counted the ones his mother had insisted their father put on the kitchen wall. He and Clyde had taken them down shortly after their parents died, but when they saw permanent silhouettes from years of nicotine stains coating the walls around the frames, they put the pictures right back up and left them there.

There were two photos on the wall: the first was from when there were three brothers, and the other was when it was down to just him and Clyde, like it remained until now. But Clyde's death didn't feel anything like it did when Bradley died, he told himself. Bradley had drowned, and was only a little boy, a baby really. Paul tried to recall his last memory of Bradley. Could he recall the day he died?

He remembered playing in the kiddie pool. They had toys in there, pool toys. Bradley toddled inside the house to get more toys. Paul could see it now as vividly as if it had happened yesterday. Bradley had Paul's new electronic car he got for his birthday. It had been expensive, the best present Paul had ever gotten. Bradley was about to throw it into the pool. No! Paul grabbed the car and tried to wrestle it out of Bradley's tight grip. Bradley clung on, working himself up into a powerful tantrum.

"Help, Clyde!" Paul yelled.

Clyde reached over the knee-high inflatable pool wall and pushed Bradley's head under the water. He held him down until he released his grip on the car. Paul took the car, got out of the pool, and went inside to put the car on a higher shelf in his bedroom. On his way back outside, he got distracted by cartoons on TV and sat down to watch. A while later he heard their mother screaming like there was no end to the sound her lungs could make. She screamed over and over and over. Little Bradley was dead.

Paul shivered. It was the first time he fully remembered that day. Always before, he could recall that he was playing in the pool, went to watch cartoons, and then their mother was screaming because Bradley had drowned. He had completely blocked out the part about the toy car, and Clyde holding Bradley's head under the water.

Maybe that was what had turned Clyde into a killer? Surely he hadn't intended to drown their little brother; he was only trying to help Paul get his car back. *Poor dear baby Bradley, poor big brother Clyde.* It was down to Paul now to do right by both brothers' memories.

After he showered and put on clean clothes Paul went directly to the computer lab. He recalled Clyde saying that the kids spent a lot of time in the lab. He hoped one of them was in there now. Sure enough, he saw the top of a boy's head behind the rows of computer monitors.

Newbie child genius Nicholas was hard at work on a private project, oblivious to Paul's appearance until Paul said something. "Nicholas, can you find somebody for me?"

"Sure, who do you want me to find?" Nicholas pushed away from the computer station he was working on and fired up a new station.

"The President of the old United States," said Paul.

"What? Seriously?" Nicholas evaluated Paul, but Paul always seemed a little daft to him, how was this any different?

"Yes. Can you do it?"

"Can Linux outperform Windows?"

Paul stared blankly. "Just tell me if you can do it."

"Yes! I can do it."

"I'll pay you," said Paul. Then he remembered what Clyde said. "And order a pizza."

Nicholas' face lit up at the mention of food. "Veggie? Extra toppings?"

What kind of kid was this? Veggie. What ever happened to pepperoni and sausage? "Whatever you want. You phone it in, here's some cash. Keep the change." He threw a substantial wad of bills, mostly hundreds, on the table in front of him.

"Hey, Paul, that's a lot of money. You don't have to do that." Nicholas studied his face. "Are you okay?"

"My brother died," he said simply. He sat heavily into a computer chair on wheels, causing it to roll backwards. He didn't seem to notice.

"Clyde? No! I liked that old guy," said Nicholas. "What happened to him, heart attack?"

"He wasn't old. He had lots of years left," mourned Paul.

"What happened to him then?"

"He got shot while saving my life."

"Whoa! He's a good big brother," said Nicholas. "You should be proud."

"I *am* proud. Find the president."

Nicholas clacked at the keyboard for several minutes and then said, "I shouldn't take your money for this."

"Take it. I want you to find him, no matter how long it takes."

"Done."

"You found him already?"

"Yes, that's why I said I shouldn't take your money. It was too easy."

"How did you do it?"

"I didn't have to do anything; someone is blogging about the pre-Big-War days. She posted all of the former president's addresses. This one says 'until present', so if she's correct, he's still there."

"Keep the money. Buy yourself that pizza."

"What are you going to do? You going to go see him?"

"Yes."

"You think he'll let you in? He won't call the police?"

"He won't be calling the police." On that note, Paul left the lab, leaving young Nicholas to wonder if *he* should call the police.

CHAPTER 20

President John Williams seethed. How could he have been bested by Ann Kinji? He stormed the halls, special agents scurrying to keep up with him. He spun around and glared at everyone in his path. "Stay away from me!" he snarled. He ducked into the restricted area that led to the underground maze of secret parking.

"But Mr. President!" protested Special Agent Billings, because it was his duty to do so, not because he particularly cared about the president's well-being. In fact, he had applied for a new detail assignment and was biding his time until he could move on.

John ignored him and quickened his long angry strides. Billings kept up with him easily, being half the President's age, and in much better physical shape. Billings signaled the team to keep up, and they too had no difficulty. The party of nine ended their manic flight only when they reached the presidential limo station. There they all stood, glancing questioningly at each other.

Billings made the decision for them: let John go alone, they'd do a convoy. He assigned his eight agents to William's impromptu road trip and returned to the White House. There was one perk to not having a bond with the Prez: Billings felt no twinge of guilt when he opted out of these unplanned ventures.

The limo driver opened the door for the president, and returned to his seat behind the wheel. "Just you today, Mr. President?" he asked.

"Yes, Jason."

"Your security detail driving separately then?" he confirmed.

John grunted. He knew he couldn't shake his own detail, but he could at least be alone in the limo. He pressed the divider button. Jason and his partner Penny were not offended, John was often prickly. Seldom was he interested in conversation. They didn't take it personally.

In contrast, President Kinji knew all about Jason's dreams of becoming a personal chef, or opening a café in Italy one day, or both. She knew about Penny's dreams to become a lawyer, and that her paycheck went straight to the Dean's office where she was attending law school, living on the cheap as she paid cash for her tuition. Yes, President Ann Kinji cared enough to listen, and she made them feel special. It is for this reason that Jason and Penny felt loyalty to her over John – it wasn't politics; they simply liked Ann more.

So when President John Williams requested that they drive him to the home of the former President of what-used-to-be the United States of America, they placed a call to President Kinji on her special line; the line she gave each of them if they ever got into any serious trouble. What was happening now was something they thought she should know about. Ann agreed, and thanked the pair of them for their courage.

Penny had made the call while still on the road, taking advantage of the privacy barrier that John himself had established. With a hushed voice, she got the message across, while John sat not two feet behind her head, completely oblivious that his nemesis had been tipped off about his upcoming meeting.

After quick deliberation with her team of experts, Ann instructed them to leave the phone line open, so that her team could record everything. They would easily clarify the sound, removing ambient noise, enhancing the sounds of the voices; all of it was fairly routine work for the team, no problem: if they were close enough to hear the conversation with their own ears – the phone would pick it up too. Both Jason and Penny agreed to get as close to President Williams as possible, two open lines were better than one.

Upon arrival, President Williams' security detail stayed outside of the former president's house, as John requested, giving him a false sense of privacy which liberated his tongue. Unbeknownst to John, the upper window of the cathedral-ceilinged home was ajar. With the acoustics of the home creating an amplifying effect, eavesdropping on the conversation between the two men was hard to avoid, and the hearing was made easier because every one of them was actively listening.

William's security detail could hear every word that was said, and Jason and Penny were in an excellent position to record everything. Best of all, ten credible witnesses were even more valuable than the recordings;

recordings that could be doctored, as surely the other side would suggest. Ten witnesses? All of them with good clean impressive records? Much harder to dismiss.

"John, long time."

"Not long enough." The former president stared into John William's blue-gray eyes; eyes that should have been deep dark pits by now, haunting him like the eyes of Scrooge's business partner Jacob Marley. But he found no sign of remorse or regret, or even awareness. Williams was no ghost of America Past come to make him repent, he was just another old man with used-up power, same as himself.

Neither man offered his hand to the other. They squared off, sizing each other up. Both thought the other was showing his age. The years had brought each of them hairlines baring more of their foreheads, more grays in the hair that was left, and more creases weathering their faces. Both men were on a variety of medications to control high blood pressure, high cholesterol, and accelerating heart disease.

The stand-off over, John walked inside the house and shut the door. "We have to talk," he said.

"Are we alone?"

"My detail is outside," said John. "What, you think this is entrapment? I'm as vulnerable in this as you are – more so, as sitting president."

The former president led the way down a marbled hallway: the house was only modest from the outside. The interior of the home was tricked out with the most expensive materials and the gaudiest displays of lighting, art, furniture, draperies, fixtures, and collectibles.

He entered the library, a room that held over two million dollars' worth of rare books and artifacts. The library was two stories high, with the top row of books nearly aligned with the cathedral ceiling. In this room, not one, but *two* windows were ajar. The conversation between the two presidents was even easier to listen in on. The agents quietly celebrated.

"John, what do you want?" he said.

"To the point, you're a man after my own heart."

"Then get to it." He settled into a chair, lit a cigar, and took a long draw. His deep red shirt, sharp, beak-like nose, and the unfortunate placement of ornamental horn-like fixtures on the back of his chair directly above his head added to the overall image of the devil himself on his throne. The rings of smoke drifted toward John like a graveside fog.

"They know about the e-mail." John did not wait for an invitation, that he knew would not come, to sit down. He selected the chair directly across from the devil, feeling no trepidation, as he was largely unaware that he was staring into soulless eyes.

"I know."

"You know?"

"I have people." The former president stroked the goatee he had grown since he'd left office. It was remarkably dark, with no gray hair at all. The contrast between the nearly-white hair on his head and the jet black hair on his sallow face was startling. The grays on his head had made his hair coarse and wild – giving him the look of a madman.

"It's all going to come crashing down. I tried to cut it off, but Kinji is running with this thing."

"It doesn't matter."

"Doesn't matter?" John threw up his hands in disbelief. He stood up to pace the room.

"It doesn't matter to *me*. I'm sure it matters a great deal to *you*, John." He folded his hands across his narrow chest. He was a tall man, of an enormous stature due to having Marfan's syndrome, a condition similar to, or possibly the same as, the disorder that Abraham Lincoln had. His arms were unusually and disproportionately long, and his overall frame was imposingly lanky. He towered above most other men. Marfan's syndrome had also given him a weak heart, which had been rumored but never confirmed while he was in office.

"You'll be arrested right alongside me. Your legacy will be that of a traitor."

"I'd do it all again. We had endless deadlock, bi-partisan bickering, lobbyists in everyone's pocket. While we were buying up weapons, kids in our own country went hungry, went homeless. Our food supply was toxic but we kept right on selling more of the poison -- while Europe banned the same stuff we served our kids for breakfast."

John groaned. "I thought I heard enough of this rhetoric while you were on the campaign trail. You don't really believe your own spin doctors, do you?"

"Yes, John, I do. I could see our America headed for ruin. There was no end in sight, what with our open borders and our out-of-control spending. We couldn't make it stop. No one could agree on anything. The old boys club got bigger and bigger. We'd been reduced to distracting people with gay marriage debates so that no one would notice that our country was dying."

"I look at you and see someone who doesn't fit in the old boys club."

"Because I represent the gay community? Is that what galls at you, John? But flaming liberal that I am, I couldn't change a thing, not even with democrats taking the majority."

"Then how can you blame my party? You had the majority."

"The Republicans wouldn't ever see reason, or they didn't care, I'm not sure which. They'd never stop throwing money on defense, getting us further and further into debt – while lining the pockets of contractors and manufacturers, over the blood of our young men and women."

"What do you care about them? I seem to recall that you cut their pay."

"Everyone has to make sacrifices. You'd stand behind the Republican agenda? Shelter the richest Americans in the world while letting the poor and the middle class wither and die, sometimes literally. Our health care went from bad to worse."

"Hey now, don't lay all that on Republicans."

"We are going to debate now, John? Not your strong suit, never was."

"Big government is not the answer. How far did liberals get with all those bailouts? And don't get me started with Obamacare," said John. "Whatever happened to *that* disaster?"

"Exactly. Nothing worked. Nothing. We were never going to agree. The Republicans manipulated the 'Christian Right' to believe that they were their party. To keep the masses loyal, the Republicans gave them what they wanted. What did they care either way if women's health care services were cut? Tax breaks to the wealthiest Americans? Why not, that's who finances the party. And I have three words for you: oil, oil, oil."

"You hated Republicans so much that you'd nuke our own country to get rid of us?"

"You feel the same about Democrats."

"Touché," said John.

"We both got what we wanted. And the country is the better for it. We were headed for complete economic ruin. There was no way out, and you know that. It wasn't a recession; it was a depression that kept on depressing. There was no way out of all of that debt. We were bankrupt. Our money wasn't worth the paper it was printed on."

"We were headed for Communism. We were already halfway there," said John.

"That's where you and I disagree, but that's water under the bridge. The country is functioning much better as a split nation, well on its way to recovery. It was time for the two ideologies to go their separate ways."

"I knew Democrats hated us, but I must say that your malice toward Republicans is impressive," said John.

"And you loathed us also. Nothing like common hatred as the tie that binds."

"You are delusional if you think we're doing better. We are *not* doing better. We are doing worse. The cost of the Big War sank us. We're still cleaning up. People are still dying or getting sick from the nuclear fallout, the waste, the contaminated water in places we didn't expect it to be. Talk about toxic food? We have much bigger problems than that now. You mentioned homeless kids, starving kids? What do you think happened when the Big War ended? You think the land repaired itself? You think it was a clean kill, and those who survived are just peachy? Haven't you seen a single podcast?" John ranted.

"The way is open for strong leadership. America can heal herself."

"With a liberal agenda of big government? Restricting freedoms until children are property of the state from birth, parental rights stripped to nothing – that is if the babies even make it to life, given that abortions are now legal even at the late stages. What's next, killing them *after* they're born?"

"That's ridiculous and you know it!"

"I see we've made no progress, and here we are with a torn, battled country littered with nuclear fallout and death."

"You should step aside, John."

"What? How dare you! You think Kinji can fix this nightmare? This apocalypse? If anything, *she* should step aside. I could repair this country much faster without her interference. But why are you going down this road? Weren't you making the point that America functions better as a split nation? Or has the truth come out: your hidden agenda was to rid the nation of Republicans!"

"Now, John, simmer down. I know you won't ever die off. You are like cockroaches. And so are your issues. Take pro-life for example. Neither of us give two figs about what happens to these women, or if a baby is a baby in the womb. Hell, I don't care if a baby is a baby when he's two. Raise them, kill them, I don't care. But don't tell me that God has tied my hands – at least we have statistics and results to back up our stand – your only argument is 'God'. But we are the same at the core. We both cater to our parties: we tell them what they want to hear. You say you care about the sanctity of life. I say I care about a woman's right to choose. The irony, or hypocrisy, is that we are both misogynistic prigs who'd sooner deny our own seed than claim it."

"I was on board with everything. I have a vigilante spirit. I actually believed that a split America would do as you said: break us to heal us. But it didn't work. And hearing you talk right now – you're crazy."

"John, you were walking right alongside me in those days. May I jog your memory – how we alone conspired to stall the debt ceiling negotiations? Deliberately letting the nation default, sabotaging nation and world markets, crippling our own government? You have amnesia?"

"The idea came after coming close to default in 2011, I wasn't the only one involved. It wasn't you and I like you allude to. We had support from both sides of the aisle."

"But John, it was the two of us who kept a cool head and had the balls to go through with the plan. The others would have caved, would have signed off at the last hour. The two of us made the play to switch sides, stalling the bill, running the clock. We had no tea-partiers in our way this time around, and after cleaning house of most of those zealots, we were home free for the big crash and burn – phase one of the plan for America to go its separate ways – a covert civil war, if you will."

"I lay awake at night wondering if we needed to take it a step further – wasn't financial ruin enough to split the union? Did we really need to let the bombs fly? We knew that the Iranians had moved their weapons within range – we could have taken them out."

"Regrets, John? I don't believe you. You and I are cut from the same cloth. I appeal to common sense and you appeal to the rest."

"You've got some serious hate going on for Christians."

"No, those poor people are only sheep to the slaughter."

"So your hatred is only toward Republicans then?"

"I wouldn't say that I don't have contempt for the Christians, of course they're a thorn in my side. They cloud simple issues with their morality, blocking my path. Not a one of them can think for himself, yet they manage to bring the machine to a grinding halt, over and over again. No, I hold no love for Christians. But I have no more contempt for them than *you* do: you manipulate them for your own political gain, pretending to be one of them, catering to their religious zeal. You don't know the first thing about their God, do you, John?"

"I see myself through your eyes and I have a strong feeling I'm going to hell," said John.

The two men looked at each other and then broke into laughter. "I missed you, John."

"No you didn't."

"You got that right."

Their banter was disrupted when they heard gun shots outside the house.

CHAPTER 21

Serena admired the photos of herself with President Ann Kinji – standing in her very own kitchen! She copied the entire 120 pictures of her family with the President onto her laptop. Then she synced it with her iPad. She made desktop pictures for each. How she wished she could post them to Facebook, but she was officially still in hiding. She wondered if her connection to the President could help her get her family's identity back without penalty – it would be so liberating to shed the Meadows persona. Then she could freely share her prized pictures of herself with the first female president!

The photos had taken only a few minutes to take, her rapid-fire digital camera beep, beep, beeping, taking dozens of pictures of nearly identical poses. Samuel raced for his own camera, and the session began anew. Ten minutes later, the cameras were off. Serena didn't want President Kinji to regret accepting her invitation to come to her home. Enough already, it was time to serve the president coffee and a snack; and, she anticipated, talk like old girlfriends! Oh, how she'd love to pick the president's brain. This would be the best coffee chat ever!

Unfortunately, that was when Ann received a call on her special line. She made her goodbyes quickly, after having spent less than fifteen minutes on the Meadow's property, and was out the door before the coffee could even finish brewing. The Meadows, clinging to their fifteen minutes of fame, stood on their lawn; watching the convoy, and waving until the president's entourage was completely out of view. Then they all trudged back into the house.

"At least I got pictures," said Serena. When she got back inside that was the first thing she did: download the pictures, and she couldn't resist sending a few to Karyn and Dan via e-mail. When she was finished gawking at and preserving her photos, she joined Tom at the kitchen table, where he was not letting the fresh coffee go to waste.

"I keep thinking about poor Clyde," she said.

"Yeah, me too," said Tom.

"I wonder how Paul is doing," said Serena.

"The secret service is probably still watching him, he's probably fine," said Tom, without conviction.

"No, they left. President Kinji said that all of her team was heading back," said Serena.

"If it would make you feel better, we can check on him," said Tom.

"I think we should do that, yes," said Serena. "I feel kind of responsible for him since we went along with his plan without double-checking to see if President Kinji really did authorize it."

"It wasn't our fault."

"I had a nagging feeling that they were lying, but I ignored my gut feeling," said Serena.

"You didn't kill Clyde. But we'll find Paul."

Serena suggested that they leave the kids at home, not wanting a repeat of the disastrous occasions of the past few days. Then they were out the door to find a person who, as recently as just a couple days ago, they had been trying to avoid. They first tried the house Paul had shared with his brother Clyde, but finding no one at home, they went to the computer lab. Serena had a hunch that he might go there to feel close to Clyde.

At the lab, they found only a young boy, around fourteen years old. They knocked on the glass window of the entrance door. He stared at them for a few seconds, dismissed them as non-threatening, and opened the door for them. He didn't say a word, but looked at them expectantly, a non-verbal invitation to speak.

"I'm Serena Wil—mmm, Meadows," she said. "This is my husband Tom. I used to be a private detective, but I've lost my knack for finding people. I'm looking for Clyde's brother, a man named Paul."

Nicholas' face lit up. "He was just here!"

"Do you know where he was going?" asked Tom.

"Yes! He freaked me out."

They waited for him to continue, and when he didn't, Serena said, "Where did he say he was going?"

"He gave me a lot of money, more money than I've ever had in my whole life! Look at this pile of money! He threw it down on the table and told me to keep it. I tried to say no, I really did. He told me to keep all of it," Nicholas' energy was that of a puppy fetching a ball.

"Why would he do that?" asked Serena. Getting information from this kid was tedious, but she had a feeling that a little patience would be well worth the effort, and boy was it effort.

Nicholas stammered and spoke at an octave that was barely audible. Serena and Tom strained their ears to hear him. "He asked me to find somebody, somebody really famous. I mean, *really* famous."

"Who?" Serena struggled against the urge to hurry the boy along, as she suspected it would only make communication even more tedious.

He lowered his voice to barely above a whisper, "The former president, before the Big War."

"And did you find him?" asked Serena.

"Yes, it was easy. I did a search and found the blog, where a fan page was and she had written about a list of the homes of all the places where he, the former president, before the Big War, had ever lived before, all of the places, and she had the one he lives in now, his current residence, and I told Paul that it was too easy and not to give me money, that I couldn't take his money, but he insisted and I still have the money. Do you think I can keep the money?" Nicholas asked shyly, hopefully.

"It's yours now, keep it."

Nicholas tried gallantly, and unsuccessfully, to suppress the big grin that took over his face.

"Did you give Paul the address?" asked Serena.

"Yes. I have it. I got it in the window behind this one, see?" Nicholas was using one of the touch screen monitors. He used his fingertip to select the hidden window. The former president's address came up, complete with a map marking the exact location.

Tom plugged the address into his handheld GPS. "Got it, thanks."

"I better call President Kinji," said Serena.

"Wow! You're friends with the President?" said Nicholas.

Serena beamed. "Well, I'm not sure I can go that far, but yes, I know President Ann Kinji."

She pressed the speed dial pre-set for Ann's special line, avoiding typing in a long series of numbers. What she got was a recording. "That's odd. It says that 'this number is closed to all incoming calls'."

"Try it again?" said Tom.

She did. "Nope, same thing, 'this number is closed to all incoming calls'."

"What do you want to do? I'm willing to go, it's up by Burnsville."

"Burnsville? I didn't know he was in the Minneapolis area," said Serena.

"Yeah, he was at the ribbon cutting ceremony at the new wing, where the stock exchange is, the financial center, where they buy and sell stocks, it was on the podcast, I saw it," said Nicholas.

"Why do you think Paul wants to see the former President? Should we call the police? Or the FBI?" asked Serena.

"That's what I was thinking!" said Nicholas.

"Then again, this isn't really our case anymore, not that it ever really was. We have only a loose connection to this," said Serena.

"Right, it's not like you're hired. It's up to you. I'm willing to go if you want to," said Tom.

"I think we should do it. Patriotic duty, right? Whatever Paul is up to, it can't be a good thing that he's gone to see the former president."

"Up to you," Tom repeated.

"They never gave you your gun back. What if Paul is uncooperative, or what if he has a gun?"

"We'll call the police."

"Good point. I'll keep trying President Kinji's phone, but… I don't feel right doing nothing at all while we wait. We might as well go up there and if we see anything alarming we can call the police."

Nicholas looked from Tom to Serena and back again. "Can I come?"

"No, but we can give you a ride home if you want," said Tom.

Nicholas shrugged. "I rode my bike. You guys better hurry, Paul is probably almost there by now." He stared wistfully beyond them through the lab door window at their car for a long second. Then he raced back to his computer station. "I'm going to watch the podcasts. I'll probably see you on the news!"

CHAPTER 22

"Hey, man, you don't have to do this," said Special Agent Whikehart. He heard Paul coming around the back of the former president's house long before Paul could see them. Paul had parked near the back entrance, oblivious to the numerous government vehicles parked at the front entrance.

It was only after he entered the backyard that Paul saw the team of agents gathered to meet him. It was then that he broke into a cold sweat, suddenly chilled and shivering. He didn't stop moving though- he walked doggedly forward, putting one shaky foot in front of the other.

"Looks like suicide by police," said Special Agent Zech.

"We should call someone in on this," said Whikehart.

"We don't have time, this guy could pop off at any time," said Gasiorowski. He stared at the unsteady figure a few yards away. Nothing about this guy seemed right.

"Call it in," said Zech.

"Meanwhile, we deal with it," said Special Agent Wooding. Wooding signaled for four team members to move in.

Special Agents Gasiorowski, Bledsoe, Whikehart and Jorissen slowly circled around Paul while Special Agent Delk called it in.

"The FBI is sending a team, but we have to keep him talking until they get here," said Delk.

Zech initiated dialog with Paul. "Easy now, tell us what you want, we can help you."

Paul stood with his arms passively by his sides, his face emotionless. He said nothing.

Zech tried again, "Why are you at the house of the former president?"

The circling agents came a few steps closer.

Paul reached into his pocket.

Agents Gasiorowski, Bledsoe, Jorissen and Wooding all fired at once. None of the shots were aimed to kill, or even to maim. They were merely noisemakers. The desired effect was easily accomplished: Paul froze, dropping what he had in his hand. No further shots were necessary.

The gun fire got the attention of the two men inside the house, and the attention of the couple who was pulling up behind the line of government vehicles parked in front of the former president's residence.

"Oh no!" cried Serena. "It's too late! We should have called the police."

"That's a lot of rounds," said Tom. "Look around; there are government vehicles all over this place. They already know."

"What do we do, stay in the car?" asked Serena. "We should at least tell them what we know. Poor Paul, he's probably dead." She couldn't see much from her perspective, but she did notice an agent walking purposefully toward their car. She shook Tom's arm to get his fast attention.

Neither was startled when Special Agent Whikehart rapped on their window. "Identify yourself, please."

Serena leaned across Tom's lap to speak out his window, "We were helping President Kinji, and Paul is part of that. We were looking for Paul to check on him. It looks like we were too late. We tried to call President Kinji on her special line, but we couldn't get through."

Whikehart handed Tom a slim gadget through the open window. "Press 3."

Tom pressed 3 and heard a click.

"Yes?" said President Kinji.

Tom handed the tiny phone to Serena. She held it to her ear the best she could.

"Yes?" President Kinji repeated, louder.

Serena held the phone up to her mouth, as if holding a microphone. "President Kinji, it's me, Serena. I'm at the former president's house. I'm guessing you already know what's going on here?"

"Yes, my team is working on the situation. Why are you there?"

"We were checking up on Paul, and learned that he was coming here. I tried to reach you on your special line but couldn't get through."

"Don't worry; we got everything we needed before he showed up. No harm done. Give the phone back to Special Agent Whikehart please."

Serena passed the phone to Tom, who handed it back to Whikehart.

Whikehart listened to President Kinji's orders via his wireless earpiece. He nodded to no one in particular, then disconnected the call.

"She's cleared you. She says if we can't get Paul out of here quickly and quietly, then we are to let you have a try at him." His voice was toneless, but he conveyed with his facial expression and body language that he didn't agree with the president's decision, and he didn't lack confidence that he and his team could take care of the problem.

Whikehart returned to the chaos in the former president's backyard, not hearing, or possibly ignoring, Serena's plea to "Wait!"

Serena said to Tom, "Are we supposed to follow him?"

"They'll come get us if they need us," said Tom.

Serena got out of the car. "He said President Kinji cleared us. I think we should go."

Tom followed suit and the two of them were quickly through the front gate, around the side of the brick McMansion, and into the immaculate, professionally landscaped, backyard. There were no gnomes or plastic flamingos, no swing sets or trampolines, no BBQ grill, no pool. There was nothing to indicate that anyone actually used this yard. Today's circus was probably the most activity the property had ever had.

"Now what! Who are they?" barked President John Williams.

Serena tried to squelch her surprise, and disgust, at the sight of Williams standing on the lawn. She answered, with impressive confidence, "I'm Serena and this is my husband Tom. We know Paul and might be able to help talk him into leaving without any problems."

Williams grunted and waved his hand dismissively. "Clean up this mess," he said to everyone in general. He zeroed in on Special Agent Wooding in particular when he said, "Give me ten minutes; get the boys ready to roll. I want to be back at the White House before daybreak."

Even though it meant another convoy, another flight, and a final convoy, the agents were relieved to hear that they'd be going home soon. They'd had enough of Minnesota. The temperatures were dropping much lower than they were used to during this time of year.

Serena waited until Williams was back inside before she walked over to where Paul was standing without moving, his arms still hanging limply at his sides, his eyes fixated on the small object he had dropped on the ground. "Paul, what are you doing here?" she said in a soft, gentle voice.

Paul snapped out of his trance then, and looked at her with clear sharp eyes. "I'm here to deliver this," he said. He reached down to scoop up the object he had dropped.

A half dozen agents' weapons made mechanical noises all at once.

Paul waved his arms over his head. "I'm not armed! I'm not armed! It's not a weapon. It's a bug. It's a bug!"

Whikehart walked past Serena to pick up the object. "What's this? It looks like a fly." He pulled the high tech insect out of its case.

"Be careful with that! It was my brother's. Clyde had it made. I was going to set it to fly around during my little chat with the former Prez," said Paul. "Hey! Stop messing with it! It's very sensitive. It can record audio from yards away. It's very valuable. I want that back!" He watched woefully as the agents passed the bug around. "At least put it back in the case!"

"They can put it back in the case, right, Agents?" Serena negotiated.

Agent Wooding brought the bug to Special Agent "The Beav" Black, whose love for spy gadgets made him an expert on unusual tech situations in the field. Agent Black's turn examining the bug ended with putting it reverently back in the case. The agents were losing interest in Paul now that they knew he was unarmed. They relaxed their stance.

"Paul, I'll ask that they return the bug to you when they are done inspecting it. Why don't we talk in the car? We are parked at the front entrance, just around there." Serena pointed to the side yard. She took a few steps in that direction.

Tom and Paul followed her. The agents gave them a look of dismissal. Whikehart had confirmed that Paul was her charge. The agents returned their attention to the two men in the house. They were hopeful that the visit was winding down and soon they'd be on their way home. Several had dates that evening that they hoped to make it home in time for.

Paul settled into the backseat of the Meadow's car. He shut the door and waited for Tom and Serena to invite him to speak. "Well, what's going on?" asked Serena.

That was all the opening he needed. "I planned to confront the former president with everything we know, record it, and give it to the White House."

"President Kinji said that they already got everything they needed, so they must have been thinking the same thing you were," said Serena. "It sounds like you can probably go home now. I don't think anyone is going to bother you."

"I see FBI was turned away," Tom agreed. "They aren't going to bring you in. You better not come around anymore though."

"I'm not done yet," said Paul. His eyes glowed with intensity, and insanity.

Serena ignored his words and ramped up her persuasion, using Paul's grief to grab his attention. "Without you and Clyde, Bryce wouldn't have gotten those files. The Angels Mark's role in this will go down in history. Clyde will go down in history as a hero. That's gotta feel good, right Paul? I know he would have liked that."

Paul said nothing. His expression did not change.

"Paul? Clyde's memory will be honored, it will. I'm afraid if you won't let us talk you into going home, we'll need to let those agents take care of you. You can't stay here," said Serena.

She tried to gain the attention of one of the agents, but none of them were looking at her. Most of the team was focused on the house, listening intently to the conversation within the presidential walls. The only two agents who seemed to be assigned to them were watching the area surrounding the vehicle, protecting them from the dangers outside the car, not anticipating the dangers from within.

"You have no idea what Clyde was capable of. He got his team to invent incredible things, Clyde's own ideas brought to life by child geniuses," said Paul.

"I'm sure he wouldn't want you to go to prison, Paul. President Kinji seems ready to let your missteps slide, because of all you and Clyde did to get at the truth. I know you think you are doing this for him, but…" said Serena.

"I *am* doing this for him. You have no idea what he's done for me. He has killed for me, he has died for me," said Paul ominously.

"But President Kinji has all the evidence we need. Justice will be served," said Serena.

"She's right, Paul. There's nothing more you can do. You need to let it go," said Tom.

"I will never let it go!" screamed Paul. His face turned crimson while the veins in his forehead throbbed.

Tom looked around to see if Paul had been loud enough to attract attention. Apparently not. At that instant, out of the corner of his eye, he caught movement. He flinched; then he laughed at his fear. "One of your bugs got out."

A tiny mechanical flying object zipped around the interior of the car, bouncing off of surfaces and dropping down, then taking off again, repeatedly. Tom and Serena watched it, first amused and then annoyed. "How do I catch it?" asked Serena.

"Oh I wouldn't touch that if I were you," said Paul mysteriously. He was now sitting with his hands neatly folded; his body strangely still and calm.

"What do you mean? Will it zap us if we touch it?" asked Serena.

"Oh, far worse than that," Paul said slowly. He grinned as mysteriously as the Cheshire Cat from Alice in Wonderland.

The mechanical insect whirred madly around and around, bumping and falling, bumping and falling. It knocked into the passenger's side window, nearly hitting Serena. It bumbled along over the interior of the car door until it bounced far enough from the vinyl that it was able to take flight again.

"I'm going to get out, and that thing will get loose!" said Serena.

"I don't mind," said Paul, a tight-lipped grin plastered across his flushed face.

Serena was a people-reader, and she took note of what she saw on Paul's face, not only his odd coloring, but the look he got every time the bug bumped into something: he flinched. *Why? Is he afraid the flying gadget will break? Is it fragile?*

No, no, that isn't it. He was bracing himself as if he thought the mechanical insect might explode when it bumped the dashboard. Her heart filled with terror as her mind clicked, clicked, clicked along until it finally understood.

It felt like the seconds were suspended, as if time stood still when Serena turned to Tom and said, "It's a bomb." She and Tom fled from the car, unintentionally letting the mechanical fly out.

Paul cackled, a high-pitched witch-like cackle. He took something out of his pocket.

"Hey! Whoa! No! Don't do it!" Tom leaped out of the car and threw Paul's door open. He tried to grab Paul's arm, but it was too late. Paul had pressed the button on the gadget and had even managed, with lightning reflexes, to set a very small joystick lever to send the mechanical insect directly into the former president's house.

"It's a bomb, it's a bomb!" Tom ran full-out into the gaggle of secret service agents, his voice hoarse and ragged as he continued to yell as he ran, "It's a bomb, it's a bomb, it's a bomb!"

"You said you were unarmed!" gasped Serena. She backed away from the car, pausing only slightly to look at the man whose madness she had so greatly underestimated.

Paul smiled. "I lied."

And with that, the miracle created in Clyde's prized lab, with intuitive flight technology, flew into the open, screen-less, window of the former president's house. Before any of the agents could respond and orient themselves to the word "Bomb", there was a sharp whistling sound, like the sound a tea kettle makes just before it blows. And then, with no harm to anyone but the two men inside the house, the world's smallest bomb blew.

CHAPTER 23

President Ann Kinji greeted Serena and Tom with a hug, which both accepted as easily as if the hug was from a neighbor, like it was an everyday occurrence to be hugged by the President.

"So happy to see the pair of you alive, well, and standing in front of me."

"Thank you," both of them murmured.

"With Paul in custody, Clyde dead, and Bryce out of the way, you won't have any more trouble. Which is why I think you should ditch the Meadows name," she said, with a sly wink.

Serena blushed.

"Of course I knew all about you. You couldn't have gotten so close to me otherwise. I know that you set your own house on fire, so that you'd be presumed dead. I know that Paul's Off-grid group gave you a new identity, and kept you successfully off the grid until William's camp came along."

"This is the part when the Scooby-doo gang tells the criminals who was wearing the monster mask," said Serena.

"Oh, I don't see you as a monster, not even of the Scooby-doo variety. You protected your family. I only wish that you and Karyn had shared that e-mail from Farideh with more than just the FBI, since our own government was not to be trusted, but of course you wouldn't have known that," said Ann, frowning, letting her words settle for a few seconds. "How could anyone have known such a thing? But now that we do, knowing that we could have taken a different course, one that would have saved many lives, or maybe even avoided the Big War altogether -- it's so hard to fathom. It was better when we didn't know. And yet, the truth shall set us free."

"It will feel good to be free," said Serena.

"Freedom is something we still have, yes. Thank God for that, agree?" said Ann.

"I'm sorry about the presidents," said Tom. "I didn't know it was a bomb until it was too late."

"I know, it wasn't your fault. Really, it was mine. I'm the one who suggested you could take Paul, going against my agents' wishes. I should have had him searched and cleared first, especially since I knew he was emotionally unstable. And he was a nut job before he was unstable. Extreme lapse in judgment on my part," said Ann.

"What's going to happen now?" asked Serena. "Will the records be buried?"

Ann's eyebrows shot up with surprise. "Of the most deadly, most massive cover-up in the history of the world? Why on Earth would we do that? Of course we respect the sanctity of human life – this is no doubt a great tragedy to be preparing for two presidential funerals, but we cannot hide from the truth. It's been buried for too long and it will not be buried with them. Their reputations and ours will have to suffer – the world needs to know what really happened."

"I admire that," said Serena.

"This opens the door to new dialog, dialog that I believe America has needed to hear for a long time. Whether or not people will be open to what I have to say,

I don't know. I'm sure to find out come voting time, which is right around the corner."

"You have our vote," said Tom.

Ann smiled. "And you have mine. That's one reason I called you in here. First, I want to thank you for all of your help."

"We didn't do much," said Tom.

"It seemed like we stayed one step behind your team the whole time," said Serena.

"You were in the thick of it all, you just benefitted from resources in high places. You'd have been able to deduce things for yourself, maybe more slowly, but you'd have done it," said Ann.

"Good thing we don't have to find out – it's over now," said Serena.

"I have a strong feeling that I'll need your help in the near future," said Ann.

"What do you mean?" asked Serena.

"Well, I don't know exactly, but I liked that you and Tom had my special number. I liked knowing that someone outside of the White House, living as a normal person, had my back. I tell you, I've lost myself here in this office. I live in a bubble, with the pressure of the world pressing on the surface of that bubble at all times. You are outside of this bubble, free to roam around without secret service agents. And I trust you. How valuable is that? I have a feeling that I'll need someone I can trust," said Ann.

"You can call me anytime," said Serena.

"I know you were a private detective several years ago," said Ann.

"Yes, before the kids," said Serena.

"I'm asking if you're willing to be on call for me. I may never call you, but if I do – are you for hire?"

"Of course. What would I be doing? Investigating outside of official channels?

"Possibly. I might need a friend."

"You've got it," said Serena, grinning from ear to ear.

President Ann Kinji showed them the door, meeting adjourned. Then she went back to her desk and drafted the speech of a lifetime, a speech she delivered the very next day, without much advance notice to the media, to the secret service, to her press secretary, to anyone. But they all scrambled and were in their places before she began.

She stood boldly in front of the flag of the former United States of America, completely poised despite the awareness that cameras were delivering her voice and image live to millions of people all over the world. Slowly and methodically, she weighed each word before allowing it to spill from her lips. Years later, her grace would be remembered almost as much as her words.

My fellow Americans, my heart is heavy as I speak to you tonight. By now, the world has heard about the death of our two presidents, the death of two men who conspired to allow America to be destroyed, to destroy us in a misguided attempt to save us; an attempt that did not work; but served to sink us further into the pit of despair, hopelessness, lawlessness, and poverty.

But those men did not act alone. Their warring ideologies were bred by all of us, by the American people themselves. From the Oval office to the Senate, from the Congress to the Pentagon, from the corporations to the small businesses, from the universities to the schools, we have held contempt for each other. May God forgive us.

Ann paused. Then she began again.

Did that surprise you just now? That I uttered the name of God? We fight over whether God should stay in, or be cast out of, money, songs, literature, even art. Why are we wasting our life's breath on this? God is love, correct? Regardless of what you believe about God, God is not the problem. Respect everyone's beliefs. Do liberals hate Christians? Are Republicans judgmental, greedy and hypocritical? There's so much hate going around and not enough love. If we keep chasing our tails like this, separating ourselves into two opposing camps, we will never come together.

Maybe if we were all more tolerant of each other, we'd have fewer government shutdowns, we'd have more food on the American table, we'd have less division. We are now literally a divided nation, but we've been polarized and broken for many years. We will never heal until we stop hating our own people. It is for that reason that I am stepping down from my party. I no longer believe that a two party system has any real chance of healing America. It is what has destroyed America.

Therefore, I am running as an Independent candidate. I will make clear where I stand on the issues, and you'll see that I probably lean more liberally than conservatively on most issues, but I'm middle-of-the-road on some issues, and very far to the right on other issues. How can a party represent any one candidate? Don't we need to evaluate each issue as it comes? Few people are so rigid that they lean to the right or to the left all the time. We humans are capable of reason and balanced judgment. Let's agree to avoid extremes!

I challenge every candidate running against me to throw down their party lines – enter this race as an Independent. Let's shake up how we do this. No more lobbyists: we cannot be bought! Let's put a moratorium on campaigning. What's wrong with using the Internet to reach voters? It's free! I challenge my opponents to live-streaming debates. All of this reform will create a mess you say? Well, it just might. And it's a mess worth making!

For the good of our dying nation, we might need to dig back into our newly-revised Constitution and tweak it many, many more times until we get it right, to re-establish ourselves as a united nation. Whatever it takes to get us thinking like rational loving human beings again – we need to do that. And that, my fellow Americans, is what's going to save us. Abolishing parties that divide us – for real this time. And most of all, learning to love our own people.

It is my prayer that the United States of America be one day united, united in her physical self, but more importantly, in her spirit. May God give us the wisdom to know what to do to heal as a nation, to become prosperous once again, to become as one nation, under God. We can heal, we can rise again – I believe that. Seek into your heart to make the changes you need to make, right along with me. Be willing to make sacrifices, be willing to think of your neighbor; be willing to love your neighbor as yourself. May God bless America.

As soon as President Ann Kinji, first female president, first Asian American President, finished her last word, the buzzing of the bees began. She answered all of the questions, all of them. She stayed on her feet, responding to every media representative from the seasoned professional, to the celebrity on-air talent, to the junior reporter. She answered questions from foreign press. She stayed on and on; late into the night. Finally, when the room grew gradually, and then completely, silent, she said good-night.

She went home, home to her imposing bedroom in the White House where Ted was sprawled out on the massive four-poster bed, snoring. Ann looked at him longingly, and even nudged his arm, but he didn't stir except to clear his throat. She lay on the bed, but could not rest. She rang the kitchen and requested a snack.

Then she picked up the phone, even though it was by now almost midnight, and hoped that Serena was still awake, and would understand.

Serena answered on the second ring. She didn't sound sleepy, but she did sound worried, "Hello?"

"Hi, Serena, it's President Kinji."

"Is something wrong?"

"No, no. I feel silly calling you, but after a night like this, a girl needs to talk to a friend."

Serena smiled warmly enough to send the feel-good vibes through the phone line. "Are you worried about your speech? It was wonderful."

"Yes, anxious. Not many people will think my address is wonderful. And I might be needing you sooner rather than later if I've made new enemies."

"Well, you're probably right. We are still polarized, and it's impossible to please both sides. But 'a wise man avoids all extremes'."

"What's that quote from?" asked Ann.

"The Bible. Ecclesiastes."

"Oh! I certainly can't start quoting Scripture. That would make both sides take offense! I pushed things as far as I could by referring to America as 'one nation under God'."

"I'm sure many were unhappy with you putting God into your speech, saw it as a nod to the conservatives probably, even though I thought it was clearly heart-felt. Liberals say they respect all views, but don't really. Conservatives say they want God in country, but aren't happy unless it's on their terms. I don't see where you can please either extreme, so why worry about that?"

"Most of us are so jaded that we find it hard to believe that anything is heart-felt, but you are right, I meant every word I said."

"Well, if your critics can't see that you are speaking from the heart, there's not much you can do. Some are so closed minded that they only hear the same things in the same way, even when someone is saying something new. Their ears hear the same old blather, and they will never stop fighting the same old arguments," said Serena.

"It does feel hopeless sometimes. In a warped way, our two departed presidents had a demented logic."

"But it's not hopeless, and at least you are trying. How can anyone fault you for seeking a balanced view?"

Ann laughed. "Oh, they can and they will. My speech will be offensive to many, many people. I might not get re-elected."

"I admire you for speaking the truth. The Emperor really is naked," said Serena.

"I'm going to have a long day tomorrow."

"Yes, I'm sure you will, but we can't be the only two people who are tired of all the hate. I mean, enough already. Don't most people by now see both sides as equally destructive?"

"We'll find out. I essentially said that both parties are wicked, are responsible for the evils in the world, and should be destroyed. I keep going over it and over it in my mind, and I don't know how else I could have said it better. And yet, I know that the far right and the far left will hate my words, and *me*, with equal passion, even after all we've been through with two presidential funerals."

"Surely there is intelligent life left on planet Earth. They just might not be in government, well, except for you."

"What did you think of my address to the divided nation, honest opinion?"

Didn't we already cover this? thought Serena. *Wow, friendship with the president is going to be high maintenance.*

Aloud she said, "Besides wonderful? Well, I think someone should have said those things a long time ago. I'm glad *you* did. The only thing that surprises me is that you are second guessing yourself and seeking someone like me out for reassurance."

"I didn't use a speech writer. I feel insecure when I've gone forward without professionals crafting and editing my words."

"Maybe you should do more of your own writing. What do writers know? Educated as they may, it's still just one person's opinion."

"True. Being a rebel doesn't sit comfortably on me. I was the girl whose report card said, 'Ann is thoughtful of others. Ann is conscientious about her work and keeps a tidy desk.' I suppose I need to get used to taking risks if I want to be a pioneer in this post-Big War world we live in."

Serena said, "Again, I thought your address was wonderful, but you're preaching to the choir. Besides, my views are probably too idealistic."

"Better to be naive than jaded, like I mentioned before – most of us have given up on ever getting past our differences. I find your views refreshing."

"I think it's more like 'view', you've pretty much heard all of my thoughts."

Ann chuckled.

"Seriously, I'm not a very political person. I don't watch the news because I find it stressful and depressing.

This is probably the most I've ever said in one sitting about anything political. I normally stay out of these conversations – I hate how anything about politics escalates into heated debate."

"You don't watch the news? Never?"

"Sometimes, not never. I know, I'm apathetic, but I don't have any faith that staying informed is possible; I don't believe what the media says about anything. And I don't believe politicians either. Except for you. So, I'm sorry, but that's all I've got. I don't have anything else to say."

Ann laughed, "I knew there was a reason why I liked you."

CHAPTER 24

President Ann Kinji waved her hand in front of the flat screen in front of her. Six hundred and seventy-nine Town Hall messages appeared. She prided herself on reading a sampling of these daily messages from American citizens every morning, after her fitness routine, and before breakfast, she skimmed through as many letters as she could in twenty minutes. She pointed at the screen to open the first message.

<<Dear Madam President,

Thank you for reversing the direction of the previous administration regarding government control of food, private farms, supplements, etc. I have a child who has food sensitivities and I need control over where our food comes from. As much as I'd like to grow all our own food, that's not realistic for me. The freedom to select natural foods that have not been restricted by government regulation is why I voted for you. I do have one issue though. You have taxed small farms and that higher cost is passed on to families like mine, but I'll take that. I do appreciate the lifting of regulations.>>

Ann smiled. The issue of food regulation had been the bane of her existence for several months of heated debate with Congress, farming representatives, and the Food and Health Administration, among others. It was good to see that her work was appreciated. So far so good, today's messages were positive. She opened another one.

<<Dear President Kinki,

I spell your name Kinki because you is Kinki.>>

Ann laughed. There were always a few trolls in the mix, and this one seemed harmless. She swiped her finger in the air to delete the message and move on to the next one.

<<President Kinji, you condemn past presidents because they rewrote the Constitution, and you are doing the same thing! Also, the idea of a Super Congress was brought up by debt ceiling negotiators back in 2011, and that is a change to the Constitution. I think you are a hypocrite. You did not have my vote, and WILL NOT have my vote!>>

Ann had heard similar rhetoric before, backlash over her recent remarks about the changes to the Constitution after the Big War. For every three Americans who wanted a reunited America, there was at least one American who wanted the union to stay divided. History had, on some level, repeated itself:

even though the union was split in two between East and West, it was the North and the South that had a division. In general, the North wanted to reunite, while a growing number in the South wanted "less government", believing it was better to stay separate.

She shook off her fears about a civil war, should she be successful in reuniting America. She moved on:

<<President Kinji, When my dog Macie was lost, I got her back because of the pet locator chip. I think all people should have these chips. You said you'd never even look at a bill to put identity chips on everyone at the DMV, so everyone has to get a chip when getting a driver's license. Why not? It's a good idea. If everyone got the chip I could find my ex-boyfriend. He unfriended me and I can't find him. If you cared about the American people you would care about this. Sincerely, Belinda>>

Ann chuckled, and then felt a twinge of guilt. This letter had a genuine voice to it. She selected "reply" and ignored the Identity Chip argument, which wasn't Belinda's real issue.

<<Dear Belinda,

I'm sorry for the loss of your boyfriend. I know there is someone new in your future. Take good care of yourself, stay busy, volunteer to help others. You'll meet the right man when you are not looking.

Sincerely, President Kinji>>

Ann glanced at the clock. She had enough time to read a few more messages. She skimmed through a collection of similar letters: cranks, critics, fans, and the occasional off-topic, but sometimes extremely articulate, political rant. She kept going until she heard an alert: a new message had been sent from a code red mailbox – President's eyes only.

Ann blinked her eyes, daring the screen to show her the message. There it was, a code red. She opened the message.

<<President Kinji, this is Penny. You might remember me? I was the driver for you and President Williams, one of the team of drivers, the one who was going to law school. I have something to tell you that I can't say in front of any of your secret service. Can you set me up with someone you trust outside of Chicago, someone who is totally unknown, with no agents. Then meet that person in some way without agents or anyone to listen. I don't know if you can do that, but I can't talk to you. They will know and they will kill me. I will send my friend to meet with whoever you want. I can't be seen with you, or anyone connected to you. Please, Madam President, there's not much time. They are watching me.>>

<<Penny, thank you for your bravery. Whatever you have to say, say it now, this is a secure line.>>

<<Not as secure as you think. They are tracking keywords. If I type anything with those keywords, they will see my message to you. Please, set me up with someone to talk to, in person. I have only a few minutes before they know I am gone. Please give me a name.>>

<<Serena Wilcox. You remember her? You'll have to travel. She's gone to Germany, of all places.>>

<<I will send my friend to her. And then Serena can meet with you.>>

There was a shrill beep: line closed.

Ann shook her head. *What could this possibly be about?* She sat and stewed about it for a few minutes, and then went to one committee meeting after another. At the end of a very long day, she picked up the phone to call Serena and give her a head's up.

Serena answered on the first ring.

"Serena? I know you're having a grand time abroad, and I hate to interrupt, but a friend of mine will be meeting with you soon to give you a message for me."

"Your friend has already found me, he's standing right here." Serena's voice sounded stilted. "But he's no friend, not unless you want me dead." And with that, the call was disconnected.

What Happens Next?

Read *Covert Coffee* (book 2)
and *Bluebird Flown* (book 3) to the final conclusion!

When the story comes to a final end,
the Serena Wilcox Mysteries continue
with a new trilogy in books 4, 5, and 6:
Project Scarecrow, *Ruby Red* and *Future Beyond.*

You can get them all in one volume in *The Serena Six*.

ABOUT THE SERENA WILCOX BOOKS

The Serena Wilcox Mysteries began with three novellas published from 1998-2000 that developed a cult following (*Gene Play, Virtual Memories, Camp Conviction*). The Serena stories evolved into a popular series of fast-paced full length thrillers beginning with book one, *Angels Mark.*

Covert Coffee (Book 2): An asset to President Ann Kinji in the past, Serena is snatched in Germany and brought back to the United States for a covert mission run by former government agents. Realizing that her participation is not entirely voluntary, she is desperate to complete the mission so that she can be reunited with her family. As the case draws her ever closer to the conspiracy to kill the president, she reaches out to the criminally insane for help, sinking deeper and deeper into a rabbit hole where the bodies are piling up and nothing is as it seems.

Bluebird Flown (Book 3): *Covert Coffee*'s dystopian, eerie, and intense vibe continues! *Bluebird Flown* goes even deeper into the madness of futuristic America; corrupt, heavy with conspiracies– chillingly close to tomorrow's headlines. As the United States continues to spiral out of control, can Serena stop all of the traitors before they kill the

President? As the layers of betrayal are peeled, will anyone remain standing?

Project Scarecrow (book 4): Serena and her crew are hired by the Gödel Solution Institute (GSI), run by former President Ann Kinji. Time travel technology is classified as top secret Project Scarecrow, but Project Scarecrow is compromised. Governments from the present and the future clash to control the destiny of mankind. Can Serena uncover who is behind this power struggle before history is forever altered?

Ruby Red (book 5): To investigate the men of the future, Serena must journey into the past. The government entities of the future are beyond sinister and they will stop at nothing to gain power over time travel technology. They threaten GSI, Serena herself, and ultimately the future of the entire planet. Why are the men of the future obsessed with the horrors of the past? Can Serena uncover what they're doing before it's too late?

Future Beyond (book 6): Serena Wilcox investigates corrupt governments of the past, present and future with her heroic crew. Serena is attacked by an evil power that manipulates her memories and uses them against her. The future of the world depends on her ability to see the difference between the truth and deception. Is Serena strong enough to fight against the evil that lurks in the future beyond? And what if the monsters of the future are ourselves?

The series continues after *The Serena Six*, with *Project Willow* and *Downward Spiral.*

ABOUT THE AUTHOR

Natalie loves all things Irish, oil painting, sugar cookies, the color red, pizza, live music, and singing. She is an author of books for all ages and enjoys people who are still capable of having an imagination, of having a sense of wonder, of feeling hopeful and full of energy, of feeling as if anything is possible, of feeling afraid of scary things and unafraid of the rest... of having courage, of being selfless, of being spontaneous, of recognizing humor, and of living life to the absolute fullest.

Natalie was born in upstate New York, raised in Indiana, and then lived in Germany for three years. She currently resides near the Twin Cities (Minneapolis, Saint Paul, Minnesota). Natalie would one day like to time travel, but for now she writes about it.

FROM THE AUTHOR

Thank you for joining me in Serena Wilcox's world. Life's better when shared! Please tell your family and friends about my books.

Watch me paint. I post videos regularly. Grab a cup of coffee and relax.

Friend me, follow me, and say hello:

NatalieBuskeThomas.com

www.ingramcontent.com/pod-product-compliance
Lightning Source LLC
Chambersburg PA
CBHW062119170626
46813CB00002B/505

9780966691962